A SH

Ned Craft, one ̶ ̶ ̶ ̶ ̶ ̶ ̶ ̶ ̶ ̶ ̶ ̶ ̶ ̶ ̶ ̶ ̶ , could remember thinking: Oh, Jesus Christ, it's Kennedy all over again!

A television camera crew was moving closer, and a woman in the crowd let out a shout. Craft turned, hoping he could find the killer out there, but remembering the Texas School Book Depository in Dallas, thought that a hunt was probably useless. He did turn back briefly to see the President's face as the car turned. Their eyes met. Craft thought he had never seen a man looking so alone, looking as if he wanted nothing more than to reach out for some stranger, to have that person nearby. The President, sick as he was, behaved as if he had become a prisoner. Yes, a prisoner. But how in this world could the President of the United States be considered any sort of prisoner?

SAM VICTOR
CUBAN INFERNO

CHARTER
NEW YORK

A DIVISION OF CHARTER COMMUNICATIONS INC.
A GROSSET & DUNLAP COMPANY

**51 Madison Avenue
New York, New York 10010**

CUBAN INFERNO

An Ace Charter Original.

First Ace Charter Printing November 1981
Published simultaneously in Canada
Manufactured in the United States of America

2 4 6 8 0 9 7 5 3 1

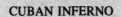

CUBAN INFERNO

CHAPTER ONE

The four sleek black, bullet-proof cars moved slowly down Second Avenue in mid-Manhattan, single file. Inside the second car, by himself, was a man who felt like a prisoner although he was actually the President of the United States.

"Damn it," Garth Crosby said, stirring some papers on the portable desk in front of him. "Damn this whole trip to hell and gone!"

He resented everything about this particular venture at addressing the United Nations. Not even the good publicity that came to a President who spoke before the international body was enough to comfort Crosby. He was in his second and last term of office, and his only interest now was to perpetuate some of the reforms that had been put into effect during the last six years. His forthcoming speech wouldn't be of any help whatever in that direction.

"The Russians," he said grimly. "And that damn Fidel, too!"

He had accepted long ago that the Russians were engaged in a long-term plot to destroy the power and world-wide influence of the United States. He had finally accepted, too, that the Cubans were among their allies. Indeed he had shocked a number of rightists in his own country by arranging a meeting with Castro only two months after being elected. He had found *el lider* to be an engaging fanatic who wasn't at all in touch with reality and felt that the United States was his country's worst enemy because American gangsters had once made Havana a playground for themselves and others. Crosby pointed out quietly that the dictator would have been better occupied looking at crop figures for cane sugar and other necessities.

The point remained, however, that Castro would periodically permit dissidents, criminals, and even lunatics to come to the United States in open boats; a practice that had begun during the Carter administration and hadn't really stopped since. The trickle had become a tide, causing difficulties to the new arrivals and those Americans who had to care for them until they could get on their own feet. And the Russians cheerfully approved of this destruction of national boundaries which was causing America some difficulty.

Now it would be interesting to see if the U.N. could be moved to express its disapproval, even if that meant taking time from its hobby of condemning the Israelis and praising those forces who wanted to destroy them by force. It had taken a few years in high office to teach Crosby the lesson that Americans and Jews didn't have any friends in the world.

The cars crawled along, as if it was almost sacrilegious to hurry in the President's presence, just as people behaved as though it was obscene to call him by some nickname or speak at all in his presence. Not everybody held with each move that the President made in doing a job, but Garth Crosby was The Man after all. If they couldn't defer to the President of the United States in his presence, most of them apparently felt, then they couldn't respect anybody.

Crowds had gathered, of course, men and women who carried signs approving of his actions in office or condemning them. Crosby chose not to look outside and get the sense of the crowd's reactions; one of his assistants would do that. He sat, glasses perched on his nose, a grim fifty-five year old man whose features perked up completely on those rare occasions when he smiled, and went over the speech to make little changes fitting his style of address, his inflections.

As ever, he had been threatened at the prospect of his making a trip. Letters had been sent to the White House—and intercepted, of course. Some of the senders had been detained until Crosby's visit to New York would be completed. Others, over the years, had made direct attempts on his life in the past and had been rebuffed by the fearsomely efficient Secret Service men, each prepared to give his life in protecting that of the President.

Crosby wished that somebody would guard him from the Washington extremists, too.

It was amazing how many experienced military men—army, navy, marines, air force—wanted to attack Cuba. Great numbers of CIA people wanted to start a revolution from within. The biggest surprise was that so few of them cared about the Russians coming in and the bloodbath that was sure to result, or that America might also be affected. Of course, more men in each department granted the need to hold off and outweighed those who wanted to charge ahead, but the numerical difference wasn't as great as Crosby would have hoped for the country's sake.

"Something has got to be done," he had said to Tal Lion when he and Tal had last seen each other in the Oval Office.

Tal was his half-brother, a young man whose father hadn't been married to their mother. Until not too long ago, Tal had lived with two girls in an airplane, but now he seemed to have calmed down enough to be satisfied with one; there'd been some bad trouble about one of his girls, as the envious President vaguely remembered. Mrs. Crosby was a quiet woman and a great help in his career, but hadn't truly excited her husband sexually in many years. The President loved Loretta Crosby, but there were times when he wished he was younger and even, if need be, a little less successful.

"What are you planning to do?" Tal had asked on that occasion some two weeks ago. He sometimes acted as his half-brother's troubleshooter on confidential problems which Crosby felt he couldn't entrust to another. Tal was a muscular blue-eyed blonde with great presence of mind and little liking for politics as such. A problem-solver by nature and inclination, it never made the least sense to him that world difficulties had to be nursed, and in some cases solutions be put off. "You're not going to invade, I suppose. Knowing you as well as I do, that seems like a safe bet."

"Lord, no!"

"Well, it's your choice," Tal said, accepting the verdict. Crosby had half-expected Tal to urge an invasion, and at the very least to suggest his own attempting to overthrow the Castro government; but the President had underestimated his half-brother, and not for the first time. "That leaves your making complaints."

"The whole administration has done that," Crosby said tiredly. "Press conferences of all sorts, television appearances, and especially backgrounders of every kind."

"Do you expect unattributed threats at backgrounders with the press to do any good if they're not carried out?" Tal was pensive, seated restlessly in one of the visitor's chairs. "I'd go even more public with it if I were you."

"The U.N.?"

"I can imagine what anybody in politics thinks of those people," Tal began.

"About as useful as ten pounds of crap in a five pound bag," the President fumed. "Small nations voting with the greatest imperialists ever known; the Russians, against imperialism, meaning us, and against the Israelis, too, of course."

"A speech might get the U.N. to look the real world in the face, if only once."

"They'd look the other way in seconds." Crosby folded his hands on the historic desk, a posture that had become known to millions who watched his infrequent telecasts; he had a good speaking voice and manner, but felt that he had more important things to do with his time. "You have no idea what the U.N. has really turned into—or I suppose you do have an idea but, like the members, you don't want to face it."

"Make a big speech and the publicity might be worth something," Tal suggested. "Better than sitting on your hands all the time."

For Tal Lion, of course, that was the conclusive argument.

"There are times, my boy, when sitting on your hands can be very useful, but I'm not sure this is one of them actually."

"It'd show the local Pattons that you're exhausting every avenue," Tal remarked.

"True enough."

Tal was reminded of something. "Have the striped pants boys in State joined the parade, too? Are they also saying you should invade Cuba?"

"I should do it myself, at the head of an army and waving my great sword Excalibur," the President said wryly. "The General Staff has a few members who are on that kick, now. The deputy director of Central Intelligence is going that route, too, which is disturbing because he has a lot of influence. And Ed Holt is on their side, of course, except when he's in the same room with me."

Holt was Garth Crosby's Vice President, added to the ticket because he was a Westerner and could corral the votes of a number of states in that part of the country. There was a muffled dislike for Crosby on Holt's part because he coveted the top spot and wouldn't get it as long as Crosby's influence could be felt. Crosby objected to the fact that Edward Holt was not a radical, feeling that any member of the right or left ideology was tolerated, but that only middle-of-the-roaders were radicals. Holt was a right-winger and every bit as dangerous and wrong-headed as the left-wing fascists and totalitarians. In his view there was nothing whatever to choose between them.

Tal's shrug indicated that not much more could be expected from Ed Holt. "Do you think that he or any of the rest of them can do you some harm?"

"Not unless they go the physical route and begin to play hardball," Crosby responded.

"Would any of them try it?"

"Not directly."

"But otherwise you think they might?"

"Well, it would break up a dull day for one of them," the President said dryly.

Not that he was amused, but it was necessary to be a fatalist about the chances of surviving.

The line of cars was on First Avenue and Thirty-Sixth Street when a shot rang out.

Ned Craft, one of the detectives in the next car, knew it for a shot as soon as he heard it, not a flat tire or a cap pistol in the hand of some practical joking kid. He could remember an incident like that taking place once when the mayor of New York spoke on the steps of City Hall, sending every dick on the scene into a fit. That recollection and half a dozen others raced through him as soon as he heard the shot and knew what it was and knew, too, that he wouldn't forget this October afternoon as long as he lived.

And then he could remember thinking: Oh, Jesus Christ, it's Kennedy all over again!

The car in which he was riding had come to a stop, and he raised the door-lock, then forced the handle down and was out of the car and on his feet in seconds. The President's car was turning the corner and he saw one of the Secret Service men inside with the President, who was slumped over his writing table. Half a dozen sheets of paper had tumbled along the small desk, some of them reddening with bloodstains.

A television camera crew was moving closer, and a woman in the crowd let out a shout. Craft turned, hoping he could find the killer out there, but remembering the Texas School Book Depository in Dallas, thought that a hunt was probably useless. He did turn back briefly to see the President's face as the car turned. Their eyes met. Craft thought he had never seen a man looking so alone, looking as if he wanted nothing more than to reach out for some stranger, to have that person nearby. The President, sick as he was, behaved as if he had become a prisoner. Yes, a prisoner. But how in this world could the President of the United States be considered any sort of a prisoner?

CHAPTER TWO

In his scuba-diving outfit, Tal Lion lowered himself through the pearly-green water to the scene of the archaeological dig.

Over the site a metal frame had been erected, and on it were mounted two cameras to take stereoscopic photographs of what was happening. The digging, as it was even called on Cape Ankh off southwest Turkey, was well under way. The silt and sand that surrounded the remains of the ancient ship cargo were being lifted gently, air having been pumped up into a long plastic tube which pulled away the debris that had acted as protection over the years. Divers ran palms over the sand covering those objects that were to be brought up. The amphora was labeled carefully, drawn, and photographed in place. Tal helped with the lifting and placing of some of the items onto an air-filled balloon over a tray that would lift the new finds to the surface.

It was a magnificent way to spend an afternoon. Tal was very careful with the clay amphorae, hoping he would see some of the next process in the early evening. At that time the material would be soaked in fresh water and then filled with dry sand to keep it from shattering. By the time it was sent to the research lab back at Texas A & M, it would be in slightly better shape than when it had been found: that is, if the Bodrum Museum of Marine Antiquities here in Turkey didn't get a piece of the action.

Tal had come out a few days ago because of a casual introduction to Dr. Warren Nunnally, a soft-spoken Southerner who was an underwater archaeologist and could talk about nothing else but his new find off Cape Ankh in Turkey, not too far geographically from the great finds at Serce Liman. In an article for the *International Journal of Nautical*

Archaeology and Underwater Exploration, Dr. Nunnally
had clarified the importance of his find. He was more than
glad to explain it for Tal's sake as well.

"The ship is probably eleventh or twelfth century and
can't be dated any more accurately at the moment," Dr.
Nunnally said, holding Tal's elbow and trying to massage it
silkily until Tal pulled away. "What we want to know is if the
ship is modern and if so, whether it's the earliest possible
example."

"I would think," Tal began quietly.

" 'Modern' is, of course, a tricksy phrase," Dr. Nunnally
said with a prissy appreciation of his own ability with words.
"When we say that, we refer to the building of a ship. The
earliest known ones were from the shell outwards—that's
how they were constructed—with planks joined and a flimsy
frame added last, my dear boy. A modern ship, as you know,
is built frame-first, starting from the inside."

Tal was interested enough to see for himself. For several
reasons he took Renata out with him, and they went by
private plane to Cape Ankh so that he could spend several
days learning about the subject. Renata, an artist, painted the
local scenes, but wouldn't put on a face mask or black wet
suit, let alone the necessary air tanks. She didn't want to risk
an injury that might keep her, if only for a little while, from
the palette, brushes, and easel.

Tal enjoyed every minute of his time below, but didn't
suppose he'd ever come back. Dr. Nunnally might have been
a man with sexual inclinations Tal would never understand,
but he was also a hard-working professional and a good
leader.

In time Tal brushed away the last of the inquisitive
groupies clustering around him, and drifted upwards. The air
compressors could be heard in time and he was soon taken
over to decompress. On the shore it looked as if the group had
been building an impromptu town of wood and concrete. Tal
went past the kitchen and outdoor dining room, the work-
room and photo lab. In one of the fragile-looking huts for
couples, Renata waited for him, putting aside her painting.

She had stopped reading a paperback mystery by Franklin Bandy and looked tense.

Tension sat badly on Renata Waye's features. A handsome woman, Renata, dark-haired and strong-featured, but not the sort who had ever been called good looking or pretty. Those complimentary terms, she had once explained to Tal, were saved for youngsters with skills expected from women: the actresses, the mannequins, even some *modistes*. Those girls may not have been smarter than a painter and in some cases didn't have as good a figure, but they were considered desirable. Renata, from her days of growing up in the town of Pauillac, on the south bank of the Gironde River just after the Second World War, the child of a German father whose last name was Veit and a French mother who had fallen hopelessly in love during the occupation of her country, was considered to be a handsome girl.

How many times had she heard Mother saying to Father, "I'm sure that Renata will be a splendid teacher for the young."

"I hardly expect her to become a wine-cellar master," Father would say with heavy jocularity in response. "Of course she'll become a teacher, certainly not a courtesan or a music hall singer."

Renata wasn't interested in that, at all. She wanted to be grown-up and live in Paris. She would then play tennis in the summer, attend opera in the winter, be married to a very wealthy man but keep the common touch by doing her own hair and perhaps some volunteer work among the deserving poor. Her domestic staff would include a butler, an upstairs maid, a personal maid, a cook, two gardeners, a part-time secretary and a handsome chauffeur. There would be three little daughters: Claudette, Charlotte, and Claire. One night a week, perhaps on a Monday, the domestic staff would be given a night out, and Renata would do the cooking for her happy family.

And instead of the elegant personage of her daydreams she had become the portrait painter, Renata Waye.

So here she was at twenty-eight, a woman who wouldn't

play at most sports for fear of hurting a hand, who arranged her own flowers and did her own hair more often than not. True enough she was able to buy from Dior and Saint Laurent and Balenciaga, but the effective clothes only helped her carry on with her life's work of showing people to themselves with the aid of paints and oils. She hardly ever wore good clothes for their own sake, but only to help her make an impression in front of a prospective subject.

She had, come to think of it, been wearing a Norell with elbow-length white gloves that night at the Veiled Prophet Ball in St. Louis, the night she had first met Talbot Lion. They had danced together and spoken briefly but warmly. She told herself that if she saw the man once more, something would happen between them. They didn't see each other during what was left of that night and the next morning. When she came back to Ibiza, where she was staying with friends, he sent a note suggesting that she might be interested in painting his brother, the President of the United States. Could she come to Washington?

Could and did. Renata, a Frenchwoman portraitist famous for her searching work, was an unusual choice for a Yankee politician to make. She went to Washington and put up with friends in Bethesda. The President's personality seemed to take form in oils under her skilled hands at their sittings. A soft-spoken, kind, but direct man, married happily. Good regular features, strong hands, alertness, great compassion.

But wasn't it odd that Tal had looked at the finished portrait and said wonderingly:

"You've painted a ruthless man!" And then he smiled. "I didn't think anybody had ever noticed."

She'd been dressed in the so-called frontier pants and old shirt she had worn to paint French President Giscard, and had been genuinely surprised at the response. She pulled back, as if her clothes were somehow immodest.

"Look at those hard eyes, the hands that are almost like claws, the way the body seems tensed forward on the chair," Tal explained. "When he sat for you, that's what you saw."

One conversation had led to another, and in time to Tal's bed and his Fornaire plane. Renata enjoyed her life with Tal Lion. Half a dozen times she had done drawings of him, but never a painting. Perhaps it was a love-token that she didn't paint him, not wanting to hurt his feelings as she might paint her true opinion about him, whatever that might be; and he wouldn't be pleased at seeing that on canvas.

Now, seeing him relaxed and muscular, at ease but alert for any indication of trouble, she wished she could paint him very quickly.

"Something's wrong," he said, coming into the hut.

"Yes."

"Tell me."

"Your brother has been—I'm sorry—shot."

"Fatal?" He was, of course, tight-lipped.

"No." Renata shrugged. "According to the radio, it is not a serious wound."

"It happened in New York City?"

"Yes. He was on his way to address—"

Tal cut in, concentrated on his own thoughts. "Garth told me he was expecting trouble from—I don't believe it."

"He was taken to Washington," Renata said, still trying to console him. "The wound can't be serious, then, if they moved him."

"I'll be right back," he said, having hardly heard.

It took time to obtain the use of Dr. Nunnally's telephone, and longer to arrange a call to Washington. The President's doctor was surprisingly uninformative. He was jarred into calling a Secret Service man he knew, but no added information was given to him. One of Garth Crosby's secretaries confirmed that the President had been worried of late and that there had been some lively talks with junior officers of the Joint Chiefs and the cookie-pusher brigade.

Everyone agreed that President Crosby's injuries weren't serious, but Tal wasn't permitted to speak with him. Orders had been issued, it seemed, and nobody knew exactly by whom. A second attempt to reach the President's doctor proved useless.

It was a grimly determined Tal Lion who rejoined Renata in half an hour.

"Do you trust my instincts sometimes, honey?"

A nod. It was sincere.

"In that case, pack your duds and brushes, because we're going to take a trip back to America. I have a hunch that there's trouble for sure and my hunches do play out more often than not."

CHAPTER THREE

Tal arranged to have the KLM jet, a DC-9, sent out to Dulles International Airport in Chantilly, Virginia. He and Renata went out by public transport, which would be quicker because of the extra time needed to put the Fornaire into shape and file a flight plan; he hadn't hesitated to use the specially equipped plane in getting to Cape Ankh, and wouldn't have minded returning in it. As for Renata, she trusted Tal as a pilot and didn't feel sure about others, but accepted what was necessary.

At Dulles, he rented a dark blue Plymouth Volaré, which wouldn't be conspicuous and was quickly obtainable. Renata, glad of the activity, asked Tal if he minded letting her drive. He didn't.

The Walter Reed Army Medical Center covers a multitude of buildings. Almost from the moment of reaching Sixteenth Street NW, the eyes are confronted by structures. Along with the General Hospital, the Army Institute of Research, and the Institute of Pathology, buildings are devoted to dental activity and research. A 50,000-watt nuclear reactor, also to be used for research, is located in one of those seventeen brick buildings. Tal didn't remember in how many medical and dental specialties the institution was accredited by the American Medical Association, but the number was formidable. As for Renata, she thought there was something almost German about the efficiency of this complex and meant that as a great compliment.

Tal chose the Georgia Avenue entrance beyond Whittier Street. Paying no attention to a brief sight of the nurses quarters or the service club or the army medical school, he hurried to the brick structure halfway between Sixteenth Street and Georgia Avenue. This was the Administration

Building, where he was most likely to get information along the lines he wanted.

He had noticed reporters pacing the manicured grounds and wasn't surprised to come up against a pair of discreet looking low-voiced Secret Service men as soon as they stepped into the building. Each came equipped with radio wires dropping from under one ear to a jacket collar; only because other government men knew Tal, had he been let to go this far. One of this pair put out an arm to stop him and Tal circled it.

"Can I help you, sir?"

"I want to see President Crosby."

"Sorry, but he's not receiving visitors."

"He is, and I'm one of them."

"You must be the optimist who got a bale of crap on his birthday and felt sure the real gift was a horse," the first one said.

"Naw, he's the optimist who—"

"Look, we can trade jokes for the next hour, but there's no point to it," Tal said. "I'm Talbot Lion. Whoever let me get this far without trouble must've told you that on the wire. I want to see President Crosby and I'm going to."

Tal's name was known to many in government circles. The relationship would have made for rotten publicity so it was kept quiet; but many a high-level government worker knew that Tal had the President's ear and his confidence.

"That's who you claim you are, but it don't cut no ice."

"Who's to say you aren't really somebody else? Barbara Walters in drag, for instance. We wouldn't let Barbara Walters inside to interview President Crosby."

Tal said quietly, "I'm going to have trouble with you two, aren't I?"

The second Secret Service man, the one with green-tinted aviator glasses, drew out a short stubby Mauser 7.63. Tal, looking down at that venerable model, heard Renata's breath draw in.

"You'd better wait for me in the car," he said to her, angry at himself for having let the overawed girl come inside in the first place.

She left without a word.

The second agent said quietly, "I'd join her if I were you, pal. Not the stupidest thing you could do."

"I'm going to see the President in a minute," Tal said quietly. "Try to stop me and I'll hammer on you. Raise that popgun and I'll kill you."

"Buddy, you're under arrest as of right n—"

A new voice that Tal hadn't heard in a while suddenly asked, "What *is* this?"

Tal turned to see the Vice President of the United States coming out of one of the rooms. No doubt Edward Holt had expected to be observed, considering the Secret Service men at his side, and had made the best of an awkward situation.

Holt's body looked fit and powerful as he moved in spite of the slow pace he took. For a man who was going to be fifty-three years old in a few days, he wasn't doing badly in the fitness department. Hardly ever sick a day in his life. Active in many sports. He was a six-footer with once-red hair that had become gray. He didn't smoke or drink much but was known as a lecher. His words, spoken in a western accent, fell pleasantly on the ear.

"Come to see the President, have you, Tal?" The Montanan asked with a wary look at the Secret Service personnel.

"Of course."

"Well, I don't know it's the best thing to do right now, Tal." Holt pushed out a friendly hand. He was said to be a persuasive man with a powerful grip. "You know the way it is in hospitals. Waking you up at dawn to take sleeping pills. All those humiliating things, like bedpans and catheters."

"Is the President—?"

"I didn't say so, just that hospitals aren't places where people really like to be seen. I visited, of course, as a matter of necessity. Affairs of state and that kind of hogwash."

He gave a man-to-man smile, which Tal didn't return.

One of the Secret Service agents said to the Vice President,

"We were trying to tell him that much, sir."

"Yes, we were only thinking of what was good for him," the other chimed in.

Tal said bluntly to the Vice President, "You're telling me that you'd rather I didn't see President Crosby."

"Not at all. Just that—well, you know the way it is, Tal. A man in hospital is given sleeping stuff and sometimes he can't think too clear."

Few statements Tal had ever heard were as worrying to him as that one. Holt was brassily telling him that the President was now ineffective, and it was enough to set his teeth on edge.

Aware that he was being watched carefully, Tal said, "I'll be able to judge that, of course, Mr. Holt. I've known him for a very long time."

"Yes, I'm sure you have." Holt wasn't deaf to the implication. "I don't mean that there's anything wrong with President Crosby's think piece, Tal. There sure isn't. But he's not himself."

"I'll tell him that you're concerned for his quick recovery," Tal said blandly, and had the satisfaction of seeing Holt flinch.

"I am indeed," the Westerner said in a fervent manner that couldn't have fooled anyone but the most loyal member of his staff. "We all are. In these difficult times, Tal, the country needs a man of proven efficiency at the helm." To one of the Secret Service men he said, "Seen any reporters hanging around?"

"They're laying for you in the press room, Mr. Vice President."

"Hm, yes." Holt composed his features so as to look grave yet hopeful. "Which way to the battlefront?"

Somebody on his staff spoke tactfully, and Holt walked off without another word to Tal.

The Secret Service man who had been holding out the gun shrugged at his colleague, then put the gun back. "Okay, Mr. Lion, but next time you might be a little more tactful." Tal thinned his lips to keep from making a heated response. The man caught Tal's reaction before he turned to lead the way to the President's room, making a point of stepping on Tal's left foot with all his weight. Tal felt a moment's pain, but said nothing. Walking carefully and favoring his left foot, he followed.

At the door the Secret Service man said to the President's military aide, "Let him in."

It was the moment Tal had been waiting for. He pivoted on the heel of his right foot, a fist cocked, and popped it across the other man's chin and just below to the neck. He had the satisfaction of seeing the bully's eyes close and a pasty gray flush cross his features before the man fell to the corridor floor. He lay still, then twitched.

"A little lesson in good manners," Tal said clearly. He turned to the military aide, whom he knew slightly, but not by name. "You heard our mutual friend. 'Let me in,' he said. I hope I've taught him that from now on he ought to say 'please', too."

"I'm sorry to tell you that the room is almost certainly tapped," Garth Crosby said quietly. He lay on his back, eyes blazing with quiet anger. Tal was reminded of Renata's portrait and the ruthlessness held in civilized control that was so much a part of it. "We can't talk in the greatest possible detail, even if there's something to tell you that I don't know of, at this point."

"Do you want to whisper?"

"The new bugs can catch a fart in a windstorm," Crosby said resignedly. "They've got one high-power bug that fits a pack of filter cigarettes, for instance, and is padded to feel soft. It even shows the ends of real cigarettes. Anybody could've left that here in the last few hours, and it's only one possibility among many."

"Do you want to write down anything?"

"No, Tal. There isn't too much I can say that you wouldn't be able to guess." Crosby smiled. He had already cursed a

blue streak and was ready to talk sensibly and to the point.
"There might be some danger to you, Tal, if you try and do
what may be necessary."

"I'll accept the risk."

"In that case, I'll give 'em a hint of what I know."

"Go ahead." Crosby's strength might give out too
quickly. "Better put skates on it."

"No, I'm all right, Tal, but I'll get to the point right now.
You remember how we talked about my troubles with the
'let's-nail-Castro-and-have-a-war-boys'."

"It'd be hard to forget."

"Yes, I suppose so. People who aren't close to this office
are sure that all a President has to do is say the word and
things get done, or not done, if that's what a President wants.
In real life it isn't that easy. People nurse their grievances and
make plans behind your back. A Vice President has his own
rooters and wants to succeed you as soon as possible."

"Holt is no daisy, I can see that."

"What I'm saying is that the plans to start a war remain
very much alive, and Castro is playing into the militants'
hands—bearding us, if you should want to be funny about
it."

"I seem to recall that the CIA tried to knock him off or
have it done."

"That was a scandal several years ago, yes." Crosby
smiled. "I can remember some of the facts and I haven't even
got a talking paper for this meeting."

Tal smiled in return. He knew that Garth was referring to
one of the single-sheets put on his desk before every ap-
pointment in the Oval Office, and that the sheet contained the
likely conversational points of the meeting-to-come—what
areas the President would have to discuss; his back-breaking
job would have been impossible without such aids.

"As for the plans to kill Castro, the CIA—this was a few
years ago, but not few enough—decided to use the Mafia as a
partner. The Mafia hoods ended up making promises, taking
a lot of money from their CIA buddies, and doing absolutely

nothing. I wish this wasn't all documented. Frankly, I'd sleep better these nights if it wasn't.''

"That I believe!''

"There were a few other schemes in the same direction, all of them nutsy. For instance, one scheme that was put forward seriously involved somebody being introduced to Castro and then setting fire to his beard.''

"I don't believe *that*!'' Tal was open-mouthed.

"There are documents to prove it.''

"All right, then I believe it. The idea is what you might call hair-brained.''

"It's crack-brained,'' the President said briskly, having missed Tal's play on words. ''That's the sort of mentality I'm up against, though, and so were the Presidents who came before me and those who'll come after.''

"Not that killing might not do us all the good in the world, if some of the things I've been told are true. Especially if Fidel's the victim.''

"No dispute about that, Tal. The bastard trains guerrillas who go back to their native countries and wait for the signal to attempt an uprising or get into some fight that may currently be going on. I shouldn't have to name all the African countries that Castro has stuck his damn nose into. No, I'd cheerfully get rid of him if I thought that his successors would be much better and it could be done without a war involving the Russians.''

"And there's some consolation, I would think, in Castro's costing Moscow more than a million dollars a day to maintain.''

"A million! Closer to three million a day, no matter what figures you've been mishearing on the boob tube.'' The President considered. Gingerly, before Tal could come to his aid, Garth reached for water. ''In the last few weeks, I've seen orders to be signed that would just about bring on a state of war and maybe impel Congress to give me one of those support resolutions that Johnson got out of 'em and cost everybody so much.''

"You haven't signed?"

"Of course not."

"Had you seen some of those orders by the time we had our talk a couple of weeks ago?"

"Uh-uh. I was preparing you for the worst, although I had no idea what form the hell-raising might actually take."

"Do you know that much now?"

"Surely." The President pointed down at his body in the hospital bed.

Tal pursed his lips briefly. "You think you were shot so that a war can get under way behind your back, is that it?"

"Yes. In the last few minutes, Ed Holt brought me some papers to sign that would've cleared the way. I kept my hands at my sides, believe me. That's point one. The second is that I made such a good target in that Caddy, somebody with a high-powered rifle almost knocked me off. Whoever did it was under orders to only nick me or wound, but not kill. Under cover of an injury like this, I might be so dazed I'd sign the necessary orders, which is putting a different gown on the same doll if ever I heard of it. That was the reasoning."

"But it hasn't worked."

"No. On the other hand, Tal, there isn't anything to keep Ed Holt from having a signature forged and cutting his deal that way. Plus which I couldn't risk national disunity by telling the truth at such a time."

Tal nodded. Of course he couldn't.

"So, Talbot, do I make myself clear?"

It was unusual for the President to use his half-brother's full first name, and a sure sign of stress. Tal considered objections.

"Except for two things, perfectly clear. How would the war get under way, do you suppose?"

"Probably by the use of some of our new weaponry. That'd give our generals and admirals a chance to test our current laser technology, for instance. We think that a beam put up with a five-megawatt laser, for instance, five million watts of electrical power, can melt an object more than five thousand miles away. The use of charged particle beams in ballistic missile weaponry could raise high holy hell with an enemy.''

''Why not try that stuff in space?''

''The money isn't there for space experimentation at this particular time, but money will always be made available for war. Plus which—I say that too often, don't I—nobody has yet figured out a proper war role for high-energy lasers, and this would be some help in such a direction. So we could try out new weapons, the thinking runs, like we did in Vietnam. It would neutralize the advantage that the Russians had when they tried out new technology subsequently, in Afghanistan.''

Tal was angered, certainly, at the prospect. He wasn't surprised though. True enough, there were side benefits to war in discoveries made for peacetime science and medicine, and it could be argued that war, in the long run, had helped prolong the span of human life. But it wasn't an argument he would have wanted to make to the parents of a teen-aged boy. And he felt that a war such as his half-brother was talking about had to be totally unnecessary; which left a solitary question.

''What do you expect me to do about it?''

''Stop 'em,'' the President said firmly.

Tal considered this. It would be the most difficult assignment he'd ever received, pitting him against some in the Pentagon, others in the State Department, and the Vice President of the United States himself.

''Do you care how I get it done?''

''Yes.'' Crosby gestured. ''Give me that pad over there.''

It was on the night table, and Tal gave it to him along with a stubby thumb-sized ball pen. The President wrote briefly, and tore off the top sheet. Tal, receiving the pad to be put back in place, tore off five more sheets and was satisfied that no deeper impression had been made by the writing. When the pad was returned to place, the President handed over the top sheet.

He had block-printed: GO FOR THE TOP DOG AND YOU TAKE CARE OF THE OTHERS. GO FOR HOLT.

Tal nodded. "Killing, do you think?"

"Only as a last resort, Tal. I don't think the resulting ruckus would be of any real long-time help."

Tal understood. Despite his contempt for politics he realized that the death of Edward Holt might be made into a far-right crusade, with people claiming he had died as part of a Communist plot and whatever else might be useful to make some current point of political ideology. He had once listened to some berserk speaker on the radio explain that President Kennedy had actually been killed by someone descending from a flying saucer and returning to it after the crime was done—a suitable punishment for that President's liberal views.

The radio! And television, of course! Tal was in the throes of getting an idea that he wanted to consider in detail.

"I suppose you'd better try for some rest," he said, making the obvious excuse for cutting short this meeting. He hadn't often avoided Garth's company since his half-brother's election to the country's highest office, but it did seem that everything necessary had already been said.

Garth looked up. "You understand the assignment?"

"Yes, you want it done without violence if possible, so that the potential troublemakers are sincerely convinced that the trouble shouldn't be started. Any idea how much time I've got? Papers could be forged in a few more days, I would think."

"Nothing's likely to happen for a while. I've alerted some of the cabinet members who are on my team in this, and I expect it'll be a week or so before any other attempt is made to get the scheme under way. They'd rather I genuinely signed such papers, you understand."

"Then you might be given sleeping pills and just before you went under, the papers might be handed over for you to sign."

"I wouldn't sign anything that way, kid," Garth said. "Don't worry. But if they want good papers that'll stand various tests, they'd require about a week to forge them. So you've got some time, but not much."

"I get the message," Tal agreed.

"Give 'em hell, boy," the President said to his half-brother.

Tal didn't see the offending Secret Service personnel as he walked out moodily to Renata in the Plymouth Volaré. She was sketching quickly and contented herself with only two or three more lines as he climbed into the car's passenger seat.

"I've got an idea for a starting point," Tal said quietly, knowing that Renata wasn't aware of the nature and extent of his assignment, or even that he had one. "Hubert Horton. He's my starting point."

Renata, as sometimes happened, surprised him. "The evangelist, you mean?" She made a face. "That one?"

"Never sass an evangelist, honey," Tal said, his good humor briefly restored by her response. "For all you know, he might have a Friend."

CHAPTER FOUR

Tal tried to reach the Reverend Doctor Hubert Horton in New York City from the Georgetown Manor on Thomas Jefferson Street, where he had registered with Renata. It wasn't any use. Cursing the need to travel as much as he did, Tal rented a private plane and pilot, then flew off to New York City.

He reached Madison Square Garden, on Thirty-third and Eighth, too late. The meeting was already under way. Horton, quietly impressive in a dark suit, a limp American flag on its stand in back of him, spoke impassionedly to the large audience.

"Is Jesus with you tonight?"

The answer came back. "Amen!"

"Is he in your hearts?"

"Amen!"

"Well, praise God for that!"

A roar of applause and amens rolled toward him until he lifted a hand for silence.

"My text for tonight," Dr. Horton said, opening his Bible, "is from Matthew 17:20, the words of our dear Lord Jesus Christ, 'If you have faith as a . . . seed, you can say to the mountain, be thou moved, and it will obey you.' Faith as a seed. Now what did Our Lord mean by those words faith as a seed?"

He was well into a sermon salted with homely allusions as he used his voice for an instrument, his hands for punctuation. Tal, impatient as he had been, found himself moved in spite of the urgency which had brought him here.

"The music of our day is filled with songs about faith in others, as we all know. But that isn't the faith spoken of by the Son of God. That isn't so much faith as it is lust. Can lust move mountains? Can a human being with his heart corroded and putrefied by lust, can he say to the mountain—''

Tal, trying to brush away the impelling quality of Horton's voice and message, was writing a note which one of the ushers promised would soon be delivered to the evangelist. Hopeful but edgy about the chances of a quick hearing, Tal sat back.

''I was speaking to my dear wife just the other day about food shopping and high prices, as a matter of fact. She told me that she had added to our food bill by purchasing vitamin pills at the supermarket. I asked why. 'Why do you that?' And Mrs. Horton told me that she'd brought so many junk foods for our three children that she felt she could only make it up to them by purchasing a bottle of vitamin pills at the supermarket checkout counter. But I ask you this question: can we, any of us, make up for our deeds of commission or *o*mission—?''

He was interrupted by receiving a note from an usher, read it, and shrugged to indicate that he was presently committed. Tal sat back even further, knowing that he wouldn't be able to drowse with Horton's impassioned and believable delivery.

The evangelist, having picked up the thread of his talk, continued a little further and then made a sweeping motion with his hands. ''Let us be charitable at this time. I would like to see every head bowed, please. Every one!''

Tal ducked his head, noticing that Dr. Horton's head was erect, the sincerity in his throbbing tones past anybody's question.

''Dear God, grant a miracle tonight. Let it come to pass that no one, no boy or girl or man or woman, no one who has heard me preach tonight, go to hell.'' On the split-second of a slight stirring from the congregants, Horton's voice was raised. ''Please keep your heads down! Now friends, neighbors, if you'll do what is right, I can help. If not, then it's possible that nobody will ever raise a finger. It's up to you.''

Silence now.

''I want everyone, every boy or girl or man or woman,

every one who believes in my prayers that you find forgive-
ness, every one to take the first move in the name of Our Lord
Jesus Christ. Raise your right hand. Good! Now put it down.
All right. If you didn't raise your hand just then and still want
my prayers, put your hands up quickly. All of you! . . .
Thank you. No, thank God!''

Someone coughed restlessly.

''Please continue to keep your heads down. Everyone,
everybody in this hall, everybody who raised a hand first.
Now is the time to get to your feet. Stand up, stand now,
stand for the Lord—They're getting up! Oh, thank God,
thank you dear God, they're getting up!''

Tal found himself wanting to rise with so many others, but
kept his seat instead. If he got closer to Dr. Horton at this
point, he would disturb the man. Tal couldn't bring himself
to do that.

''Now look at me, those who are standing. Look at me,
please—This is the night for God to deliver you from tempta-
tion and wickedness, to make you free. I have here a place
where you can come and stand. I'll pray for you, I'll help you
back to God. Please take this course, please in the name of
Jesus take this course, and come to this place here—They're
coming, thank God! They're a-comin' down every aisle! Oh,
God is good to us tonight. See what God is doing. Open your
eyes and see!''

Tal, with most of the others, looked up. Prayer advisers
were walking among those who stood with bowed heads. Dr.
Horton bowed his own head and prayed for them. A gesture
to an adviser caused that one and others to begin handing out
literature and New Testaments in paper covers.

''Bless you all, brothers and sisters in Christ,'' Dr. Horton
said. ''For those who are among the afflicted, who are in pain
and suffering, I will try to ask for the help of God through His
son.''

The faith healing would soon begin. Those supplicants
with illnesses were directed to form a line going down the
spacious right-hand aisle. The healing line soon stretched
raggedly, almost the auditorium's length, its members quiet

except for an occasional sob from a woman's throat. The
prayer advisers filled out oversized white file cards, taking
down information swiftly but legibly. Others in the audience
were directed back to their seats.

Tal, knowing he was being an opportunist but seeing no
other way to make progress quickly, was in the middle of the
line.

Dr. Horton threw a glance behind him, causing the choir-
master to bring out a chair and a microphone shortly afterwards.

"Now." A tired Dr. Horton was sitting on the rectangular
dais nearer to the supplicants without being on a level with
them, and everyone became quieter except for a baby. "In a
few minutes I'm going to start praying for the sick. Before
that, however, let me say one thing more . . . Your attention, please! I was about to say that I have to make one point
clear to everybody. I am not a healer. Please remember that
Hubert Horton is not a healer. I have no power to heal
anyone. I am not a doctor or scientist, not a miracle worker. I
cannot heal. I am only an instrument, a humble instrument, a
humble instrument in the hands of God. It is God who does
the healing. It is God who heals in the name of our Lord
Jesus. It's not Hubert Horton who heals. Hubert Horton
doesn't heal."

He looked at the bottom line of the first card given up to
him. The full lips suddenly seemed drawn tight in sympathy.

"Diabetic, are you, sister? Do you take orinase tablets?
Insulin?" The woman nodded. "I'll pray for you, sister, and
we'll hope for the best. Do you know that Jesus loves you?"

"I—I do." The woman's voice quavered. She must have
been in her fifties, carefully made up and turned out. "I do."

"Say it loud, sister. Say it for all to hear. Don't be
ashamed of the love of Jesus."

The woman drew a deep breath, swallowed and said more
loudly, "Jesus loves me!"

"All right, sister." Horton put a hard hand on her
forehead, using so much pressure that she had to pull back
slightly. "Dear God, in the name of Your son, in the name of

Jesus Christ, I pray that this woman be made whole again and that the illness of diabetes leave her body for all time.''

His face seemed to draw tighter in the moment's silence, lips thinning, eyes narrowing. His features had smoothed out when he took away the hand. A moment passed before he spoke again.

"I believe that something may have happened there, sister, but I'm not sure." He was controlling himself to keep from saying more, from making a definite claim. "Please go to your doctor before you discontinue medical treatment. If you don't have any further trouble for a year from today, write a letter to me in the town of Eula, Missouri, and let me know that. God bless you, sister, and may Jesus always be in your heart."

Dazed, the woman stumbled out of line. A prayer adviser took her hands and led the way to another aisle. Three front rows had been cleared for people coming off the healing line, and she sat slowly, hands shaking. She looked down in bewilderment at herself, as though some change had occurred in the shape of her body.

Horton's voice was soft, dealing with others. " . . . Do you know that only God can heal? Do you accept it that only God in the name of Jesus Christ washed in the blood of the lamb can heal? . . . In the name of Christ, the name of the Holy Ghost, the name of Your son, I ask You to spare this man from pain and misery. Heal him! . . . Leave this man's body, you damnable illness! Leave it, I say!" One woman hurried forward from the healing line and kissed Hubert Horton's hand, first the back and then the meat of the palm.

Tal was feeling thoroughly ashamed of himself when his turn came. Horton, looking even more tired, glanced at him, nodded and said quietly, "You wish to speak with me in confidence?"

Tal couldn't have spoken at all at that point. Horton, far from rattled, led him to a point further up the stage. The faith healing evangelist's voice was ragged.

"After the healing I have to pray for the healing line members and then for everyone in the hall. I'm tired and

devoutly hopeful that I may have done some good tonight or
still be doing good. You've come to interrupt me. Tal, I owe
you an important favor and admit that, but you're using up
every ounce of credit you may have or want with me."

"I'll accept that much, Dr. Horton." Tal had saved the
evangelist's older son from a scrape that could have cost the
boy his good name, and had the tact not to remind the
evangelist indirectly by asking after the boy's current welfare
or that of others in the older man's large and happy family.
"This is vital business."

"I ask you for mercy's sake and my own, Tal, to keep it
brief."

"Here goes, then. You're a good friend of Vice President
Holt's, and—"

"I officiate at an occasional prayer breakfast for him and
other government officials when I can, yes." He blinked.
"Indeed I plan to do so again this Sunday."

"Will you give a sermon at that time? Good. I hope you'll
give one against the folly of starting wars. It may not be
useful, but do it and keep this talk a secret."

The evangelist's eyes had widened with sudden under-
standing, and his tone was quietly respectful. "There must be
something else you want if you've come to see me now.
Something urgent."

"Yes, and I can't get it except from somebody close to
Holt. The Vice President lives with his wife in Georgetown,
but he has an apartment in Washington proper. I've heard that
so often I believe it."

"He uses it on those nights when he's only able to get a few
hours sleep. One of the rooms is like a gym."

Tal wouldn't dispute that with a friend of Holt's, but it was
well-known that the Vice President of the United States had
more than just an eye for good looking women who were
political groupies.

"Where is this other apartment located?"

Dr. Horton hesitated. "Can I ask why you need this
information now?"

"I'm afraid not."

The faith-healing evangelist pursed his lips, then shrugged. "Very well, then. Ed Holt has an apartment at the Watergate on Virginia Avenue near the Potomac River and Kennedy Center."

"I know the place." For a while, the entire country had known about the location and of that illegal break-in by Republican Party hired men into Democratic campaign headquarters, leading to the discovery of the high crimes directed from the Nixon White House itself. In a way, the location seemed appropriate.

"Thanks, Dr. Horton," he said to the wary older man. "And I hope you'll forgive this interruption, but it was the quickest way to get important information."

The evangelist, forgiving Tal with a nod, kept him a moment longer. "And how is your brother?" He was one of the few men out of government who knew of the relationship.

"I think he'll be better in a little while," Tal said, adding sincerely, "thanks in part for what you just told me."

CHAPTER FIVE

A friend he hadn't seen for a while lived two blocks from the Garden, in what was considered a business district. Adrienne Long's apartment was big enough so that Tal could take a room to himself and use the phone, and be sure of privacy as well. He called Renata at the Georgetown Manor and gave her instructions, carefully adding that she didn't have to follow them unless she wanted to. Renata, probably bored at having been alone this long and interested by an adventure that didn't involve any harm to her, took the phone numbers he gave and decided on what dress to wear after making the phone calls, when she'd do Tal's bidding. . . .

Putting down the phone, he walked into Adrienne's living room. She was busily mixing a Desert Cooler for him, a drink he had liked when they'd been going out, and he could smell the Southern Comfort clear across the room.

"Staying over?"

Tal shook his head. "Sorry."

"How come you're not staying?"

Tal never liked coyness in women, and wouldn't lie in return. "I asked my friend to do a job for me, and I'm damned if I'll laze around while she's working."

"It never crossed my mind that we were going to laze, if you want to use that word."

Calmly, Adrienne smiled at him. Under the burning red hair was angel-white skin with a touch of rouge showing on cheeks and the backs of hands and shoulders; a New York style that he had never seen before. It occurred to Tal that he knew the girl's body, with the hips that didn't seem bony, and her age as well; but knowing that much and little else about the model was to know almost nothing about her.

Not much more than he had known, basically, at the start. They had met because she was one of the girls who posed

with President Crosby in a publicity photograph that certainly
seemed ill-advised in retrospect, and Tal had been called to
see his half-brother on that day. He and Adrienne had taken a
week together, and then another two months after and that
was all. They had parted with expressions of genuine friend-
liness on Tal's part and regret on Adrienne's.

Now it seemed that she apparently wanted to take up where
they'd left off.

"You can wait for me in the next room and I'll be right in
there," she said. "Even a quickie will remind you, Tal, of
what you're missing."

"Honey, you asked me the reason for leaving now and I
gave it. That's really all I can say."

"Well, I'm afraid you won't be able to count on this place
as a crash pad for long, Tal. I've had a marriage proposal
from somebody you probably don't know, and I'm planning
to accept it and amble down the aisle in December."

"Lucky man," Tal said, and wondered at his capacity to
say with sincerity things that he didn't feel at all. She had
probably just decided to accept after seeing Tal's reactions to
her proposition and decided that she wasn't growing any
younger. He kissed Adrienne, wished her a long and happy
life, then left.

The October night was hazy rather than cool, and Tal had
the luck to see a cab at the curb. No driver was in it, though,
and he took it for granted that the man had slipped into a bar.
The only one in sight was located across the street. He found
himself on the outer edge of a mass of human traffic, men and
women crossing two ways, and moved gingerly. Odors of
frying meats and fish dismayed him, but in this era of instant
food their pervasiveness wasn't surprising.

He took a right turn and paused under a lightly swaying
sign with a pig's rear end painted on it. A pub, no less. Veddy
British. Past the half-open door, he strode along the dark
room with its wooden tables and chairs. Colorfully dressed
men and women were sitting around in idleness. A burly,
round-shouldered man looked up at him, a glass of beer in his

heavy hand. He'd been staring out across the street, where that cab was parked.

"Your hack over there?"

"Uh-huh." The driver finished his beer, then got up. "Sharp of you to find me, pal, but that's what I heard about—" a pause "—New Yorkers."

Tal wondered if the pause hadn't covered the man's realizing that he ought not to speak Tal's name. He decided, watching the man wipe his lips with the back of a hand, then saying, "Pardon my French," that he was becoming paranoid. Just a good-natured slob, this driver.

"From out of town, are you?" Tal asked idly as they walked to the cab.

"Chicago, by way of Terre Haute, as a matter of fact."

"Can you find LaGuardia Airport?"

"Climb right in." He made a slightly bored motion with a hand.

The cab wasn't a medallion job, which bothered Tal only slightly. He didn't see the driver touch the meter and realized, too, that no price had been mentioned for this trip. That last omission would have been disturbing to anyone who knew the ways of New York City drivers, as Tal did. He closed the door and locked it on himself, wary and wondering if this hadn't been some elaborate setup after all. There seemed a reason for Tal's paranoia now, but he wasn't going to cut and run when he might still be a hundred percent wrong.

The driver made a turn, going in the opposite direction from LaGuardia and northerly. Tal could understand such a maneuver for maybe a few blocks, certain as he was that every driver had his own little con games; and sometimes the traffic itself was a pain. But this driver continued for longer than necessary, even for a con game. He would accept Tal's suggestion, making a correct move, then go off the route again. They were close to Wall Street the second time it happened, a business district abandoned for the night.

Tal asked quietly, "What's the scam?"

"I don't get you, mister."

No further delay was possible. "Stop the cab or I cut out right now, and you don't want that."

The driver did stop, his face changing from dirty white to a mottled red as he turned. "Pay up," he said, pulling to the curb of a deserted street. "That's thirteen dollars and fifty cents you owe."

Tal understood. He'd refuse to pay, and there'd be a fight in which Tal would possibly get the worst of it, depending on the driver's preparations in advance. If he paid, this driver would find some other excuse for a fight.

"Are you planning to get rid of me before I can do a job?" Tal asked quietly.

"All you got to do is pay up," the driver snapped. "That's eighteen dollars and thirty cents you owe."

Tal knew he had better make plans for the trouble that was sure to come. He kept his fists behind the front seat's shoulder.

"So you want to stiff me, is that it?" the driver asked menacingly in the pause.

Tal didn't see him reach for the blackjack unless it had been on the seat behind him; but he was aware of the opening door and a swift kick that smashed into his groin. He doubled up, unable to breathe for a second except in jagged spurts. Another blow hardly mattered, even as it crashed against him. He couldn't do anything but gasp, unable to hold his breath and let it out, to move or keep himself in one place.

The further blows had come swiftly. He was outside the cab. Through eyes swimming with moisture brought on by pain, Tal saw the driver duck, and felt a light jab to the chin as if he was being set up for a punch in some boxing match. Now that Tal was nearly helpless and barely able to stand, the cab driver was bent on showing that he was a sportsman. It was ludicrous and painful, both, and Tal told himself not to lose consciousness as he staggered after another punch.

There was a streak of profanity followed by a surprise punch aimed with a foot at Tal's crotch. It missed and gave excruciating pain just above the right knee.

At that moment, when it was the last thing he wanted, Tal felt his lids slowly closing as he dropped to the sidewalk. He knew it would be disastrous to lose consciousness, and the driver would now get to work and inflict injuries that would need more than a week's recuperation. For instance, a few blows with that blackjack around Tal's head. . .

It didn't happen. He had fallen on a sidewalk crack, and the pain knifed through him, causing him to feel alert. His eyes flew open at the unexpectedness of it. The pain itself kept him from losing consciousness. He heard a mocking laugh and saw the cabbie reach over to skull him for sure.

The threat galvanized Tal and the suddenness with which he was able to move took the driver unaware. The man pushed himself forward and then Tal gripped him fiercely by a leg. He would never know where the strength of desperation came from, but it was part of him. He started to twist the leg, determined to break it. The driver, distracted from the mayhem he had planned, called out and then shouted. Tal showed no mercy, not even letting go when he heard a terrifying snap in the man's leg and an accompanying shriek.

The driver's distress accomplished what Tal's hadn't—a small crowd. No more than half a dozen people, some drivers who'd stopped their cars, pedestrians leaving their jobs later than usual, were watching.

"Let him go," somebody called, but didn't make a move to stop the fighters. Nor did anybody else. Tal wouldn't have been surprised if he was being directed to release the unfortunate cabdriver.

"Drop that blackjack," Tal managed to say.

"On your head I will," the driver insisted through hard and painful breaths.

"Here goes the other leg, okay?" Tal said, and reached for it.

He didn't have to. The lead-tipped blackjack thudded to the sidewalk and the driver hurried brokenly into his cab. There'd have been no point trying to get the license plate number as Tal felt sure it couldn't be traced.

"Need any help?" a passerby asked, moving forward now

that there was no sign of trouble.

"I feel great." Tal got up with his own strength. He was fighting waves of dizziness and nausea that rose and vanished one after another. He held on to the wall of the nearest building, moving very slowly, one foot in front of the other. He paid no attention to the questions about what had happened and whether he had the driver's number. "Never better in my life."

CHAPTER SIX

Renata put down the phone when Tal was finished talking, then looked at the pad in front of her and picked it up again. She made two calls, introducing herself as Tal Lion's friend and phoning on instructions from him. She was believed for the simple reason that those particular numbers were otherwise hard to get. By the end of phone call number two she had learned that Vice President Holt was in his Washington apartment for the night, and that he was working.

She dressed carefully, picking light colors that gave her a cheerful look and accented her figure. It seemed to Renata that being with Tal could be considered good for her shape, which had improved in these last months. When she was between boyfriends, her figure went slightly to seed, which sometimes made it harder to find a man she could like and respect.

Disdaining the rented car, Renata took a cab out to the Watergate. There was a half-moon, and the Virginia Avenue building looked as if it was the color of butterscotch. Lights seemed to cover it, adorning every window, each about the same size, with blinds and drapes to hide the innards of each room from prying eyes.

Renata took a deep breath, pulled back her shoulders, and walked in. The doorman, behind a desk and with a bank of television sets at his back, looked up brightly.

"Who do you wish to see, ma'am?"

"Mr. Passy."

"Mr. Charles Passy, the columnist? Just a moment, please." He phoned swiftly. Renata just had spoken to the well-known political writer a few moments ago and had gained permission to use his name. "Thank you, sir." And, to her, "Third elevator to the left, Miss."

She had to ask him a second time. Communication with
this fellow could be difficult over the long run.

Knowing which apartment she really wanted, Renata first
took the indicated elevator and then walked a flight down.
The halls were slim but gave the impression of spaciousness.
Everything looked as if it was brightened by sun. Here and
there she saw a chair, a table, and some undistinguished
paintings in dark and serene colors. It surprised her to be able
to hear voices behind certain doors.

She touched the doorbell of the one she wanted. A young
man appeared at her side, a little out of breath, having been
loitering near the fire exit. He wore a dark suit and couldn't
have been past thirty. Renata wouldn't have liked to paint
him, which was her standard for judging anyone.

"This must be the apartment I want." She pulled out the
piece of paper on which she had written the number of the
Vice President's hideaway.

"I'm sorry, Miss." He spoke well, but had that air-
pinched-back-in-the-nostrils tone that bad comedians as-
sociated with the French.

"Well, let me talk to whomever answers the door and
perhaps I can make headway with him."

"You probably can," the young man smiled, confirming
Renata's judgment by taking pleasure in the double meaning
of his words. He looked Renata over.

Some need to share that joke made him turn almost ap-
preciatively as the lock was clicked backward in the door. His
lips gave a St. Vitus twitch and he touched his breast pocket
handkerchief if only briefly, hand near the heart.

"This lady came to the door and rang before I could stop
her," he began.

"Any good lookin' lady is welcome," the Vice President
said, and grinned. Renata didn't like Edward Holt, but felt
that she'd be interested in painting this sturdy, athletic man.
Like so many politicians, close-up he seemed to be younger
and more vigorous than his photographs in newspapers or
magazines, let alone the television image. He was probably
in his mid-fifties, with silver hair, and a western accent that

was used to disarm people. Mr. Edward Holt was well aware
of his skills with most women and his ability to win over
many men.

"How can I help you, Miss?" He listened courteously,
head cocked. "No, you've come to the right apartment
number and anybody who misled you deserves not to see you
tonight. Come in an' we'll get to the core of it."

He gave a little bow that was more than an inclination of
head and shoulders, then stepped to one side. Renata found
herself keeping from a curtsey, and said nothing. She walked
in as he edged away, wondering if Tal had known what he
was up to in sending her here, wondering why Tal thought
she could persuade this man to tell or hint more of some
important matter than he might of his own free will. She was
good at opening people up, heaven knew, and it was part of
her work; but the Vice President wouldn't want anything like
that done to him and he was what the British called a "down
cove."

"We'll phone downstairs in a few minutes and find the
correct apartment," Holt said. "But meanwhile you must let
me give you a drink."

"No, thank you," she said with a primness that begged to
be contradicted.

"One measly drink won't do any harm, and it gives me a
chance to pour for myself in company. Right nice company,
too."

"Well, I suppose it'll be all right. And after all, I do know
who you are."

"Yes, I'm sure you do," he smiled.

He spoke to the Secret Service man, very quickly and
quietly. None of the words were clear. Renata knew English
well, and it seemed hard to believe that he was talking at a
normal speed. The Secret Service man turned to go, his shoes
ruffling hairs on the carpet.

"You look like a Scarlett O'Hara type," Holt said.

"The storybook girl, you mean?"

"No, no, the drink. Ain't you ever been to New Orleans?
They mix a lot of 'em out there and you look like the type

who'd go for that particular brand 'a firewater."

"I'll try it, then."

The bar was at the northern end of the room and the Vice
President busied himself with lime, cranberry juice, whiskey
and cracked ice. The drink was colored red, with a creamlike
froth on the top. It was gratifying indeed to have had a drink
mixed for one by such a high official in government, and she
supposed it was one of the ways in which an elected officer
might gain the goodwill of some others, as well as other
favors from time to time.

He was preparing a stinger for himself when he suddenly
said, "I'm going to need crème de menthe. Hold everything,
I'll be right back." No doubt he was on his way to tell the
Secret Service man to bring up the refreshment, and specu-
late briefly on his chances for making it with her at some time
during the evening.

Time passed, and she found herself looking around, at first
because she felt that there was history to be seen in this room.
Papers lay on the table, anchored by weights, and others were
push-pinned into a framed corkboard. All of these held her
attention. She gave less than a minute's consideration to the
colors and textures of the room, all picked by some shrewd
interior decorator. There was a Moroccan grilled screen,
Italian chairs and a polychrome wood angel, a Chinese portrait, and an abstract oil done by somebody who probably
painted with Swiss cheese, as well as brass-latched lacquer
and reed trunks.

Getting up gingerly she approached the table, having decided that she'd claim she was only looking if by any chance
Holt returned too soon. The typed papers had seals on their
tops. Renata supposed that it was small notes she'd be looking for, probably handwritten. She looked down and a jagged
writing caught her eye. Reaching out a hand, she stirred it.
The writing was too small for her to make out at this distance,
and she had to raise the paper.

She hadn't heard the room door opening, but was aware of
a certain crispness in the air. She looked up, seeing hostile
eyes measuring her. The cold dislike in those eyes, framed by

a ruddy complexion, was astonishing. And then she remembered that he had looked forward to dallying with her and possibly a brief conquest. Instead he realized he had been set up. No wonder he was controlling himself only by main force.

"I ought to cream you right now," said the Vice President of the United States, with a politeness cold enough to raise ice streaks on the far side of hell.

"I was just looking around."

"Is that so?"

She had hopes that she could talk herself out of this trouble. "Certainly it is. On my word of honor."

"I know that you forced yourself in here by claiming you'd made a mistake," Holt said. "I had my bodyguard phone downstairs and he told me you had asked to see some political writer, some *sneak*, who lives here."

"It was a misunderstanding, then, and I got the apartment number wrong." She was able to face him and speak quietly. "You'll get nothing with threats."

"I'll get nothin' anyway," Holt snapped. "You didn't come here to have a little fun," and she gathered that other females had done just that, making any excuse to find themselves in the Vice President's chambers. "You came here to do some spying."

"You think that I am a Russian spy?" She had to laugh.

He heard the sincerity behind that laugh. "I think—I know—you're a friend of Tal Lion's."

"What?" This was something she hadn't expected. It made her wonder why Tal had exposed her to this danger. Only by an effort of willpower was she able to keep from calling out.

Having watched Renata's mobile features the Vice President said quietly, "I saw pictures of the unveiling of the painting you did of the President, so I know who you are. What did you want here and why did he send you? You're still with him and you wouldn't come here otherwise."

She shook her head. Holt moved so quickly that she was unprepared, fingers around her neck and squeezing tight.

Screams faded to gurgles and her feet kicked out. No sounds were coming from between her lips by the time Holt pulled his hands away.

Breathing almost as hard as Renata, who had lost her balance against the corkboard, he bellowed, "Well, what were you supposed to find out here?"

"I—I don't really know." She spoke hoarsely. "Anything that might be of interest, that's all he told me. I swear."

"And he knew what was most likely to be on my mind."

"I—I can't say anything about that."

"For the moment, I'm inclined to buy it," the Vice President said grimly, studying Renata's expressive features. "But Tal Lion expects you back and I suppose that if you don't return right away he'll come here. Good. Get up and sit on the couch on the other side of the room, baby. I think we've got some waitin' to do, and a bad surprise for Mr. Busybody Talbot Lion at the end of it."

CHAPTER SEVEN

Much as Tal hated commercial flying, he was usually able to sleep on one of the flights he occasionally had to take. This time he was dreaming. An old man was explaining that he hadn't left his house since William McKinley was assassinated in '01, but it hadn't hindered him. "My invention will single-handedly save humanity," this old buster was telling Tal. "It hasn't been easy, what with spiraling labor costs and the rotten way they make everything nowadays." It turned out that the old buster had invented television, guaranteeing people at home that they'd be too busy to fight wars or riot or do any of the things that made other people unhappy. "Any day I'll be ready to transmit pictures of Milton Berle, and all this to insure a peaceful civilization."

Tal woke up laughing and grateful for that much. He remained bruised from that set-to with the New York City cabdriver, but felt refreshed and calm as the plane touched down at Dulles.

He phoned the Georgetown Manor as soon as he got to the terminal building. No response. Tal wasn't surprised. He knew perfectly well that Renata was at Holt's and that the Vice President had more sense than to have harmed Renata, even if he understood why she was really there. Besides, he now had a good excuse to barge in and a witness who had been able to make an entrance and would hear the conversation that was going to take place between them. If Renata had by any chance given herself away, Tal was sure that no harm could have been done.

He couldn't help feeling leary about hiring another cab after that business in New York City, but took one at random. The cabbie expressed no surprise at Tal's having no luggage

and Tal didn't say a word after giving the destination. He and
this cabbie were establishing a good working relationship.

He had no trouble getting into the Watergate, asking to see
Passy. The writer confirmed over the phone, as agreed in
advance, that Tal was expected. From then on, Tal took the
same course that Renata had, and found himself confronting
a Secret Service man at the Vice President's door.

"What can I do for you, sir?"

Tal considered. "I'm going to get inside to see the Vice
President, partly because he's got my girl friend in there. If
you've been told to stop me, then you're going to have big
trouble. If you've been told to let me in, on the other hand,
then there's a chance we might become lifelong buddies."

"Your name, sir?"

"Talbot Lion."

"I've heard that name," the Secret Service man said in
neutral tones, and added surprisingly, "I think I've seen you
at official functions."

"If you want more proof of who I am," Tal said, reaching
into a pocket for identification.

"Not necessary, sir. I've got a good memory for faces."

He rang the bell twice. The door was opened by the
powerful-looking Edward Holt, who was dressed in a dark
gray suit, a Countess Mara tie slightly widened at the throat.

"I've been expecting you, Lion," the Vice President said.
He opened the door wider, then turned. "You can leave now,
sugar."

Tal saw Renata sitting on a couch at the far end of the living
room. By the position of her body he could tell that she was
under more stress even than he might've expected.

"Did Holt put a finger on you, Renata?"

"More than that." She added, "But he didn't rape me."

Tal, restraining himself but making a mental note for the
future, said only, "Stay there, Renata. I have a lot to talk
about with him, and you'll be interested in hearing it all."

Holt glanced out at the Secret Service man, considered,
then closed the door and backed away from it.

"Your girl knows nothin' of what's on your mind in

coming up here," Holt said. "Better for her sake to keep it that way."

"I'm not sure I agree about that." Tal took both fists out of his pockets, but held them in place. "You have a lot of guts, Holt, closing the door on your protection after what you did to Renata."

"That happened as part of a conversation we were having." Holt sighed. "A nice gal you've got there. Loyal as hell, I don't mind saying, and you didn't even have to marry her."

Tal joined Holt in the living room, which seemed to him nothing more than an eye-hurting riot of colors. He sat down next to Renata, briefly taking her hand.

Holt said, "Let's have somethin' clear between us, Lion. As long as Renata is here, I'll deny whatever point you bring up."

"Then I'll make it short. I know that you and some Pentagon people are planning an attack against Cuba and an all-out war if necessary."

"*I* don't know that."

"Okay, you and the Pentagon are making plans to start such a war against the will of the current President of the United States."

"Are we indeed?" Another remark had surged to Holt's lips, a nasty one, but it wasn't spoken.

"There's a witness to this talk, and if anything does happen along that line I'll bring Miss Waye to the offices of the *Washington Post* and they'll spread this story over their front pages. And the rest of the country will take it up. The Watergate scandal is going to be nothing by comparison."

"Have you spoken your piece now?"

"Yes." Tal said. "I'm willing to go with Miss Waye. I think I've said and done the most that is possible."

"One thing you haven't done," the Vice President said quietly, appearing to inflate with menace where he stood. "You haven't seen one of my many sportsman's collections."

Tal blinked, startled. "Is this a gag?"

"Judge for yourself." The Vice President turned to the door and opened it on a large room with bare floors. On the walls was a collection of unsheathed swords. "Great, aren't they?"

"You're not planning to attack Castro with a sword!"

"No," Holt said pleasantly, inclining his head and opening his gray eyes wide. "But I'm planning to go at you with one."

Tal looked briskly at the man. He seemed in full possession of his five senses, but there was a glint in his eyes that hinted of hatred.

"It takes a pair to play that game," Tal said, avoiding the trap even while he seized the bait. "Assuming I'd want to."

"You've probably read that dueling is a hobby of mine," Holt said. "Wouldn't expect that, I suppose, for a Westerner. You'd think it would be guns and horses. Well, I like those, too, but I'm fascinated by the *code duello* and everything about it. I suppose because it makes me feel like a sophisticated continental warrior and not just a cowboy from a wooden cabin." He spoke firmly again. "Now what we can do is to let you out of here with your promise to keep quiet—but I won't believe it. So you help me have a little exercise for the day. If there should be an accident to you, why, that'd be too bad."

"And in case I won't? What then?"

"I'll pick up a sword and take you. By the way, if anything happened to you all the same, I'd put another sword in your hand before calling the Secret Service man. We'd have been exercising and there was a bad accident. That'd be the official story."

"And Renata?"

"She'd be reasonable about it after I got done proving to her why it was necessary."

Angrily, Renata said, "I'll scream. I can be heard in the hallway—"

"By my bodyguard, who has no key to the inside," Holt said. There was a glint in those otherwise dead pupils. The

Vice President was looking forward to dealing with somebody who didn't have the least experience in swordplay.
"Now pick the one you want, Lion. You have no real choice
whatsoever about participating."

Tal surprised the other by smiling. "Yes, I think I'll do
that."

Renata gasped as Tal strode into the bare gymlike room
and drew a sword off the wall. It was heavier by far than he
had expected, but he didn't doubt he'd be able to manage the
damn thing.

"A Ricasso," the Vice President said, shedding jacket,
shirt, tie, and undershirt and dropping them neatly in a pile in
the southeast corner. "I'll take this other one, myself."

Tal observed the zero-over-T stamp of Toledo, of perhaps
the finest workmanship, on the base blade.

Only the continuing glint in Holt's eyes testified that he
was well aware of Tal's inexperience with the sword, let
alone the tiredness with which he came to this duel.

Tal had eased the sword down and stripped to the waist
now, himself.

"Am I going to have a second?" he asked, remembering
some dueling scenes from the movies.

"*I* won't, so why should you?" Holt countered, not un-
reasonably. "At the first wound, of course, the victor will
step back and the fight is over."

Tal knew, of course, that the Vice President had nothing
more in mind than to give him (and Renata) a bad shaking-up.
In Renata's case, he was certainly succeeding. If Tal hadn't
been already tired because of the extra traveling and the
dust-up with the New York cab driver, he would have been
interested in this stunt. It was so damned out-of-the-ordinary,
to say the least.

Holt was looking almost clinically at Tal's chest and midriff, as if planning to run him through.

It crossed Tal's mind that Edward Holt could very well
forget himself in the thrill of dueling an enemy, and go out for
more than just scare tactics. Tal didn't remember that any-

thing stranger had ever happened to him, and supposed that
Renata was nearly paralyzed. Better not to look in her direction and avoid a possible surprise rush from the enemy.

"There'll be a doctor on the scene very quickly in case of
need," Holt said, emptying his pockets while Tal did the
same. Everything was being done out of the order that
might've been expected, perhaps Holt was so excited or
angry he could hardly organize it properly. A rotten sign.

"Let's not waste any more time on this foolishness than we
have to," Tal said, hoping to draw anger.

" 'Foolishness'? We'll see." Holt sounded aggrieved, as
if one more damned unfair advantage had been taken of his
good nature.

Tal wanted to say that centuries ago, this whole business
had been a form of murder ritual though called an affair of
honor. He decided to concentrate only on what was happening in front of him. Plenty of time for deep thinking later on.
Hopefully.

The Vice President of the United States called out, "En
garde!"

Renata drew a deep, jagged breath.

Holt, following the rules Tal didn't know, raised his
weapon so that the guard would be level with his chin, and
brought it smartly down; he'd have been able to strike back
swiftly if Tal had suddenly lunged. The man was in good
condition, arms muscled but not so much so that a woman
might consider it ugly. His heels were together as part of the
opening, feet at right angles. He put one leg in front of the
other, weight shifting to the right leg as he made his opening
thrust on an unprepared opponent.

Until that moment, when the Toledo steel whistled past,
the day and night had been difficult but not grotesque. Now,
with a sword thrust that left almost a musical note in its
steam-filled wake through the air, Tal accepted it as possible
that he might be killed.

Renata screamed, which helped further to bring him to his
five senses.

He knew now, instead of only suspecting, that the Vice President could very quickly be carried away. Seeing a chance to get rid of an enemy, he might take it and not care about the possible consequences. A certain amount of his movement was play-acting, to give Tal a bad shock and keep him emotionally off-balance. (Who would he tell this to, and find himself believed? Not even Renata's supporting testimony would be of the least help.) To this extent, Holt had succeeded. Tal, who'd have previously argued that he had experienced danger in all its possible forms, had known nothing at all like this.

And if he should do any harm to Holt, he would himself be in trouble or ineffective from that time on. Part of him wanted to tear Holt apart for having hurt Renata. There was no way to come out of this with a whole skin unless no damage was done to either contestant, and Tal saw no possibility of managing that. It probably wasn't something he could control.

First moves, in spite of his lack of experience, offered no problems. The enemy blade came toward him and was parried with a block. Another thrust from Holt, and Tal made a beating movement at the lower shield of the Vice President's rapier. Holt had to pull back unwillingly, giving Tal those few badly needed seconds to draw himself together.

Holt smiled, though, encouraged. It was plain to both of them that Tal remained strong, but far from overpowering; the last twenty-four hours had taken their toll on him. He was a sportsman and had killed in his time, but he wasn't at peak strength and there was nourishment for only two sides of his nature in this bout.

An attack. A successful parry—and Tal found himself caught in a redoublement that scraped part of a shoulder without drawing blood.

But it must have seemed to Holt that Talbot Lion was barely holding his own. Holt confidently launched a running attack, and Tal made one swift stop thrust that worked, and followed it with others. Holt pulled back for a straight thrust,

disengaging. Tal was grateful for the breathing space. He had
tried one or two devices, not knowing that they were standard
in dueling with buttoned foils or without; and he had succeeded. There was room for hope.

Holt suddenly squinted as he came forward, concentrating
more deeply. Tal, looking for a moment into those depthless
gray eyes, saw murder in them.

Tal set himself carefully now, dreading more of feint-
and-attack until he grew too tired for a defense. Instead, he
kept himself so close to Holt that the swords clashed. Again
Holt pulled back, maddened by the frustration. He hunched
his shoulders, getting ready to throw his skill against Tal and
the turned-up sword.

Tal saw a possible opening for himself, a way to win. He
was thinking with split-second common sense, but knew just
how much he stood to lose.

Swiftly, Tal took two steps back and thrust out with the flat
of his sword hand across the lower shield guard of Holt's
Toledo steel. The sound made a sting in the air. Holt's sword
flew out of his hand and whirled him half-around.

He tried to lunge for it, but Tal kicked the weapon to his
own left. Holt took one faltering step in that direction, then
realized it was hopeless. Taut-lipped, he stood, looking with
hatred at the witness who kept him from further violence.
Holt was well aware that Talbot Lion had given back as good
as he got.

Renata's gasps and dry, husky sobs turned into sighs of
relief. Holt glared at Tal and at her, then turned from both of
them. Defeat wasn't a condition he was used to or accepted
easily, not in sports or politics.

"Get out of here," he said quietly. "Both of you get out."

Tal, having caught his breath, said, "Remember what I
told you. If that attack on Cuba starts up, there'll be black
headlines about you up and down the country and a long
investigation that won't do you the least good."

Holt threw his head back. "You can't stop anything from
happening, Lion, nothing at all."

At least they understood each other. Tal didn't see or know just how much more he could have accomplished and hoped that Holt might be speaking out of bravado when he really did intend to trim his sails. The time was long overdue, though, to leave this place of unexpectedly whirling, deadly blades.

"Thanks for a memorable evening," Tal said quietly.

He wasn't exaggerating at all.

CHAPTER EIGHT

Crane Rickert arrived from Cuba with a number of other refugees, thirty to be exact. He and the twenty-nine others were huddled together in a small boat with some eighteen thousand feet of space. In this vessel they had sailed the warm Atlantic to the Straits of Florida and Key West.

The refugees found themselves and their presence accepted, but not welcomed. Rickert, although he was sunburned and spoke Spanish well, could have told them that he was an American by birth, and that he knew at least one fellow American who was very high in government and could vouch for his honesty in that matter.

Crane Rickert kept his mouth shut through the processing at Eglin Air Force Base on the Florida panhandle. He accepted his momentary fate, sleeping in one of the rows of cots in a pair of plane hangars. He watched tall pines being chopped down to make room for even more housing, and didn't say a word, either. He glanced down at his meager belongings in plastic bags and pillowcases, and clamped his lips shut. A *compadre* told Rickert that he was going to be sent to another camp on the edges of Tamiami Park, but he said nothing. He showered with dozens of men, ate his K-rations and was grateful for them, and recognized a Castro spy and complained against that one—in Spanish, which was translated by a harried clerk. He accepted forty dollars from the Cuban Patriotic Junta, which was supposed to be a help to him in this inflation-ridden country of his birth; and was grateful for it, too. He accepted clothing which had been donated by the same group.

But in all this time, receiving the kindness which could be

expected from one Cuban to another, Crane Rickert kept his
mouth tightly shut.

And for a very good reason.

Only a few years ago, Crane Rickert had been an American
citizen and on top of the world. Twenty-five years of age,
with a good public relations job, a recent divorce, and already
finished with that wild post-separation period of swinging
with girl after girl. He had settled on one of them and saw her
steadily, a redhead named Sandra Nyefeld.

He had taken her for a ride in the sky-blue Opel that a
promise to pay had brought, and talked about the co-op on
New York City's Sutton Place that a bank loan would make it
possible for him to buy. At no time was it obvious that a trap
had been set for this muddled young guy who hadn't yet
found his footing after an emotional upheaval. There was no
way he could have guessed at the trouble he'd be bringing on
himself so shortly. Establishing a line of credit, as he had
done, was damned important in a P.R. job, proving that the
fellow was a with-it, top-chop man. Before he could have
said eighteen percent per annum, he was being offered credit
in department stores, banks, even cat houses.

All he had to do was nod or smile and whatever merchandise he wanted would be his. Crane Rickert found himself
with goods he'd never have touched at all, otherwise. Did he
really need that TV recording equipment when all he ever
watched on his boob tube was the Jets or night baseball?—
and then only if he was home in the first place. He had a
friend named Tal Lion with a half-brother who was deep into
politics, and Tal took to that equipment in particular. As for
Crane, he felt an irresistible need to prove that he was on top
of the world and could have anything he wanted.

Credit had its built-in catch, as he knew, but didn't completely appreciate. Only a small bite had to be paid every
month, but it could add up to a mint of money. Everybody
could lay off some of the interest on Uncle Sam at tax time,
but it was a high interest rate nonetheless, and put together

with the cost of the goods themselves it could be backbreaking.

He was heading for a fall, and when it came nobody could save him.

Two dozen checks must have gone out during a one-month period before Crane realized that he was laying out a fortune for what he didn't need or really use. Coming on top of alimony and two sets of lawyer's fees, it was only a matter of time before his skimpy but hard-earned savings went up in flames.

Like a fool, he started trying to give back some of the merchandise. It couldn't be done, except in a few trivial cases. Then he tried reselling what was left, but without getting much money. He was still paying in credit for some merchandise that he had already gotten rid of at hefty losses. So-called credit counsellors lectured him severely on the perils of overextending himself, but not one of them objected to being paid by credit card. As he said to Sandra a little later on, "It's a wonderful life if you weaken."

Enter Mr. Waterman.

Crane never remembered his first name, although he was to see it on many checks. Waterman phoned one evening, an officer of Cash-for-Credit, Inc., a highly respectable firm and not one of those three-dollars-for-two loan shark outfits. Mr. Waterman was simply in the business of lending money to middle-class people who might be temporarily embarrassed.

Crane's problems were solved. Outstanding debts would be paid from Mr. Waterman's overflowing cornucopia of money. He'd have to worry about nothing except paying back with interest some time in the future.

Now that another source of money was firm, bills started to add up even faster. Tal Lion tried to warn him, but changed the subject when he saw that Crane was worried but not able to help himself. By this time, Crane had bought himself a closet full of sports jackets, one for every minute of the day, as Tal said. And Crane developed a liking for orthopedic shoes, although his feet had always been strong as iron. After all, Mr. Waterman was seeing him through from one month to the next.

And then he couldn't pay a month's installment. Waterman's lawyers sent a few nasty letters. Crane realized that he had picked up a major problem. Arranging a bank loan was useless. Another respectable money-lending outfit gave him nothing but an interest-free lecture.

No wonder he was upset and angry when he got back to his job one May afternoon. He had taken time for a gym workout at Prexy's—all major credit cards accepted. Naturally he'd been flexing his muscles for an hour or so, and it took no real work to give the glutes and pects a few more flexes.

In that mood, Crane went to a meeting to talk about a new promotion for Chippewa Protection Systems, Inc. A highly-placed member of the firm was holding forth as Crane entered hurriedly.

". . . By the middle of next year I'm in hopes that there'll be a number of Chippewa systems to offer. We expect systems that will be linked electronically to monitoring stations, with electronic screams and special alarms. Given simple penlight batteries we can produce a system that'll temporarily blind any intruder."

One of the secretaries came in and was waving a note which she put into Crane's hand.

". . . Sensors can give off microwaves with ultrasonic waves or light waves. Let those waves be disturbed, and the circuit breaks and trips the alarm. Of course there have occasionally been some drawbacks to the system."

The note said clearly that there was a process server waiting to see him in the anteroom, and that the man wouldn't wait forever.

Taking a sudden great interest in the subject of alarm systems and wishing he'd had a built-in one himself, Crane asked, "What are those drawbacks?"

"You could start up an air conditioner and break the alarm circuit," the executive said grimly. He was a heavy man in his forties, and always seemed to be thinking about something else. "You could turn on an electric light in some situations and break the circuit. Even the so-called automatic dialer that calls police on the same general principle, as you may know, ran into so much trouble in California that it was banned after the police kept getting one false alarm after another. Nevertheless. . ."

"Yes?"

"The products have to be fixed, somehow," the executive said. "We've made the decision that Chippewa is moving into these new fields. There's a gold rush on, and we don't want to stay out of it. Your job here, of course, is to put the product over with the public whom we've never disappointed."

Crane was going to point out that selling defective merchandise wasn't a good way to make more friends with the public. He didn't have time. A door opened swiftly and a hard-looking man strode in and glowered at Crane before approaching him.

"Son-of-a-bitch," Crane said, made furious by the unjustified interruption. He went tearing after the man. Luckily Crane didn't fracture the process server's neck or back, but did dent him a little. The process server, however, called an officer to put Crane under arrest.

Certain that his job was lost and that a pyramid of debts was going to smash everything it had taken such a while to build, Crane was hauled down and booked. As vividly as a hand in front of his face, the end of that talk with the desk sergeant came to his memory.

"Mr. Rickert, you're going to be sent up before a judge who'll determine bail against your nonappearance in court on the trial date. Can you show that your address in the city is permanent?"

"I can."

"Then you'll only have to make arrangements with a bondsman to be out of here in a short while."

"I'm not certain I could pay him, ah, right now."

"Don't you have a checking account?"

"It's empty, ah, right now."

"You're employed by Lucas and Eldridge in what seems like an important job. A man who's situated that way doesn't have to worry about money in hand."

"Do you mean—?" A wild surge of hope had risen in him. As it turned out, for once he was justified.

"Mr. Rickert, I don't see any problem at all. There isn't a bail bondsman in the city who won't cheerfully accept one of the major credit cards."

Crane understood. Credit had got him into a mess, and it was credit helping him out of it.

Far, far out. For he had decided once and for all to get as far away from Creditville as he could go. Pressure had forced him to assault some man who'd recover soon enough, and he didn't want to find himself doing anything like that again. As for the wheelers and dealers who'd urged him on to disaster, they'd have to make their fortunes without help from him. What had to be done was to make arrangements where he'd be able to start a new life for himself, a life without credit.

The English-speaking countries and Europe were ruled out immediately for the purpose. He took a LAN-Chile plane out to Santiago. From there he flew to Havana.

Public relations jobs couldn't be had, but he had always spoken Spanish well, and managed to drift from one spot to another. He finally took a job in a variety store. He worked hard, kept his nose clean, seeing a woman once a week.

The only bad turn he'd had came when the boss asked to see him one afternoon. Crane had the pleasure of hearing Señor Sagrera tell him that the business was being expanded and he would be appointing Raoul, as Crane now called himself, to a new position. He would become the store's first credit manager.

Crane could have lived with that and shared two rooms with four other people as well; but he found himself more and more disturbed by Fidel's so-called danger law, *La Peligrosdad*. Anybody considered dangerous, for whatever reason, was jailed indefinitely. That was a condition he *wouldn't* accept.

Hoping that conditions might change, Crane waited out the

first large-scale emigrations during the Carter Administration in Washington. Later, when Tal Lion's half-brother became President, Crane decided that if anything in his life needed squaring away it was Tal who might be able to help him do it. They hadn't kept in touch, but he and Tal would be friends in spite of the time that had raced past.

Crane had been in his native country for a month before he realized that he was putting off getting in touch with Tal. Common sense said that the White House would be able to offer some information on Tal Lion's whereabouts, and it then became a matter of scraping together the money to put through a long-distance call.

He got some of the information he wanted, but no address or phone number for Tal Lion and only a hint that Tal was currently in Washington. Crane Rickert was sweating when he put down the phone at last.

His next problem was that of getting away from Eglin Air Base. It would take a few days, maybe, but he felt sure he'd be able to manage that much.

CHAPTER NINE

Tal woke up with a sickly feeling, probably brought on by yesterday's schedule of moving around, the fight with a cab driver, and the joust with—yes, with the Vice President of the United States. He and the sports-loving Edward Holt of Montana had dueled, and Holt had certainly tried to kill Tal to keep his mouth shut. He hadn't dreamed it.

He turned away, bone-weary, from Renata sleeping soundly next to him. It seemed impossible that one night had passed since then. Generally he could recuperate considerably faster from a rough day. He supposed he was slowing, and it showed.

He groped his way along the side of the room, not looking at anything else but the bathroom door. Once inside, confronted by the mirror image of a man whose eyes had seen everything, Tal found himself beyond caring, beyond hurling curses at his bad luck. An older guy couldn't sensibly expect things to work out the way they would for somebody full of piss and vinegar. He felt fuddled with gin, but knew he hadn't been drinking.

Renata had already gotten up. One piece of evidence of his increasing slowness came to mind: would a younger Tal Lion let a girl sleep undisturbed at his side for a whole night? Especially a handsome girl like Renata Waye. Not a chance, dammit!

She had gotten breakfast set. Tal faced down his o.j., bacon and eggs, coffee and toasted English. As he was plainly in a grim mood, Renata kept from making aimless talk. She waited for his first restless stirring.

"What do you plan on doing today, Tal?"

"Reporting to the President."

"Is there that much to report, do you think?"

He recognized the echo of his own doubts. "Honey, I'm not sure."

"You think that Holt may have said he'd pay no attention to what you want as a sign of—what is the word? I know it in three other languages, but not English. Oh, yes. Bravado. A sign of bravado?"

"He might have been keeping up a front, sure. Besides, Garth himself might have some other ideas if he's in better shape today."

"All you can say is that you might have been successful."

"Right."

Nobody bothered Tal when he parked the Volare and walked up to the Walter Reed Army Hospital Administration Building. He strode along the sun-brightened hall, only to be stopped by the sound of an impersonal and unfamiliar voice.

"Sir?" A middle-sized young man had strode out from a cluster of three others, stepping aside swiftly to make room for him. This one was dressed in gray, with a dark-trimmed pocket handkerchief and a varicolored Dior tie. His skin was liverish, and his tentative half-smile showed yellow-stained teeth. He had dressed a dissipated body in good clothes.

Surprised, Tal asked in turn, "Are *you* Secret Service?"

The man started to draw out identification. Tal, who knew how easily such credentials could be forged, shook his head. He balanced his weight between both legs, hoping there wouldn't be any trouble but feeling prepared to meet it in case of need.

"My name is Talbot Lion and I'm here to see the President."

"Yes, Mr. Lion. Will you wait a minute, please? I'll check it out."

Tal would have expected these men to carry miniaturized walkie-talkie equipment for such communications. Maybe some regulation had been just issued against using those machines in a hospital corridor, or the use was in conflict with a hospital rule. He had seen so many oddities in his life that he didn't often draw quick conclusions.

He nodded that he'd wait, and the man walked off, leaving two others. One of these, he now saw, was in a policeman's uniform. Tal couldn't decide if that was phony or not. They spoke quietly, but the voices carried along the corridor. Tal could make out every word.

"Are you here without that partner of yours?" the man in plain-clothes asked. "You two guys always work real fine together, you and what's-his-name."

"We asked for separate assignments."

"How come? Oh, it must be your missus, I bet! Probably kept tellin' you that your partner was working against you and you started to believe it. Well, whosis was the best partner you're ever likely to get."

"I don't know if that's so."

"The other guy's wife must have hammered on him, too. Wives have loused up more good working police than upside-down working hours or free drinks at the nearest bar."

The uniformed man, judging from the quick look Tal gave in his direction, seemed embarrassed.

"Take my advice and go over and talk to whosis again as soon as you get back from this gig," the man in plain-clothes said earnestly. "See if the two of you can't get together. And the next time your missus starts in on you for being a cop who has to work by himself and against his own partner, tell her to shove it."

Tal didn't know if these men were also genuine or putting on an act for his benefit. If they were anything but government men, he couldn't help wondering how they might have gotten into this place and how he could find out.

Patience wasn't one of Tal's strong points and he was glaring at the door to the President's room. It seemed no wider than six thumbs end-to-end. Probably he could—

A girl in nurse's uniform came out of another room, looked at him, blinked, and smiled as she came over. Uniform or not, she showed a head of blonde hair falling gracefully down to the back of her slim neck. She was shorter than Tal, and slender except for the goodies outlined under the sturdy linen uniform.

"Mr. Lion? I saw you here yesterday. Are you coming to visit the President again?"

"Yes."

"Come with me, then."

"Don't you have to clear it with those guys over there?"

"I know you and that's good enough," the pretty blonde said, smiling. "Mickey Anson is my name. Michelle, actually, but I've never been formal."

"All right, Nurse Mickey." He lowered his voice. "Those guys—are they Secret Service people, do you know?"

"I suppose they are." Nurse Anson had lowered her own voice in response. "They certainly are authorized to be here, and their papers passed muster with our people."

Tal hoped for the best, and put off any decision about the matter.

The President looked tired-eyed, worse than when Tal generally saw him. Seeing him again, Tal remembered that he had their mother's self-satisfied lips and eyes, but resented the heritage of his father's thick nose. Where Garth was commanding, Tal was likely to show an agreeable sense of self-mockery that came from his youthful desire for hurry, for promptness, and for fair-dealing with others.

Tal propped one of the visitor chairs up against the door, aware that the tired-eyed Garth Crosby watched.

"My doctor has dosed me with something and I'm likely to cork off pretty soon," Garth said, looking at his brother. "Talk quick and to the point."

"Well, about the particular job—"

"Be direct. I'm probably bugged here, like I told you the first time; but it's better to have the enemy know I'm on to them."

Tal detailed what he had done. Crosby stopped him at the first mention of faith healing.

"Have you turned into a believer?"

It wasn't relevant to the biggest worry, but Tal answered. "The people who go to Hubert Horton's services believe in it, and we've all seen some strange things one way or another."

"A few hysterics convince themselves they feel better, and sometimes the cure lasts for as long as one week."

"That's better than nothing. And Horton believes in it, I'd swear."

"That's his problem." Crosby smothered a yawn, and Tal realized that his half-brother had been thinking distractingly of his own aches and pains. "What else have you done that makes some difference?"

Tal discussed his meeting with the Vice President, adding that Holt might get rattled enough to call off others who were planning the all-out invasion of Cuba.

"Holt is nutty about dozens of sports," Garth added, having heard about the dueling episode. "I'd heard he duels with some friends, using real swords; but I never believed he'd try to settle a score that way. The moral is that even if he can pick up votes for you, never run a crazy bastard as Vice President."

Tal appreciated the restrained sympathy, but kept to the point. "I suppose it's possible that he'll stop the others from going through with what's on their minds."

"Oh, it's possible. Either that, or he'll try and have you killed." Garth spoke with a breathtaking honesty that Tal had always admired. "And see that it's done, too."

"I'll be careful."

"You'd better be careful enough. Nobody wants you cut to pieces, Tal."

"Of course if I was crippled then I'd be getting a public pension."

He had meant to be ruthlessly funny, like Garth Crosby could be, but the words came out badly. In the mid-morning October light, Garth's eyes looked small; but he dominated the room and the discussion by his political importance as well as the depth of his speaking voice. Even in silence, though, as Tal had noticed before he rose so high in political circles, Garth Crosby was imposing.

Some impulse made him go on. "If something does happen, you'll be rid of me for all time, and if it's bad enough the government will be saved a lot of money."

"Worried, are you?" Garth threw back his head, but the laugh was weak. He ran two fingers along the nostrils of his parrot beak. "Don't blame you. It's a hairy business, and I've tried to make some progress from here myself."

With wary eyes, Tal asked, "Doing what?"

"I've talked dutch-uncle to some of the JCS people. Admiral Honeyman says he's got no information and I believe him. As for Klemmert, my secretary of defense couldn't find his ass with both hands, but he's competent and will lie his head off to his own mother for my sake; but he won't lie to me. He says he's got no information about this caper, and I believe him."

"And Harry Cotton?" Tal asked. The director of the CIA was somebody with whom he had worked in the past, and whose word he would be inclined to take.

"Well, CIA is bugged up as usual. There is a very powerful wing of members who feel sure that Russia is getting the best of every interchange with us and that the only thing to do is strike back violently. That wing has a lot of clout, but isn't likely to act until they've got others in their corner who haven't been there recently."

"They might have just that, by now."

"Yes, they might. Harry admits as much."

"So what he's doing is to pile guesses on top of other guesses."

"Just about. But if he comes across even the slightest hint of any problem in that direction, he'll act quick and ask questions afterwards. I've got his word on that." He smacked his palms in anger mixed with sour laughter. "And you know nothing can go wrong because everybody's expecting it to."

Tal, who sensed that he was in for more trouble than he had experienced in all his years, decided against telling Garth about his fears involving the Secret Service guards in front of the door. It'd be too much, on top of everything else.

"In other words, you think there's a very good tipoff: if I suddenly get creamed, then the operation is all systems go. If I don't, then there's nothing to worry about. Except for me, of course."

"Tal, I think you should have a guard," the President said.

"I don't."

Garth Crosby bit his lower lip. He knew his half-brother better than to pursue the matter, but decided he would put somebody on Tal's back as soon as possible. He only wished he didn't feel so sleepy. Damn the doctor for filling him up with a powdered lullaby, and damn himself for having taken it!

Tal started to get up.

"Wait just a minute," Garth said.

"You'll be asleep in no time," Tal said, as his brother's eyes closed weakly. "If I get out now, it'll save you having to try and make believe."

"Goddam it, Tal! Just when I need every ounce of stamina I can get together."

But Tal was waving a hand as he approached the door, having turned his back on the sleeping President.

He opened the door to the corridor which wasn't occupied by anybody; that much had to be a sure sign of trouble. He had a split second in which to decide whether he should close the door on the President or on himself so that he'd stay in front of the door till somebody got back.

The decision had to be made swiftly. If anyone was gunning for him, it would be better to keep away from the room. He closed the door on himself and was in the corridor before the hospital room of a wounded President of the United States. Against all the rules of the United States Secret Service, nobody else was there.

A moment passed before he became aware that a blur of

sounds was taking place out of his view. A door suddenly
opened and the pretty blonde nurse, Michelle Anson, came
rushing out toward him. There was concern etched on her
features.

"Mr. Lion, Mr. Lion, I've just found out that one of the
men we thought was—"

She spoke no further. At her right, coming along a turn in
the hall, the well-dressed Secret Serviceman with the bad
teeth appeared. Tal started to say something, he never knew
what, and then the so-called Secret Service man had pulled
out a gun from its holster and was shooting. The nurse,
Michelle Anson, pulled a palm to her heart. With a queasy
and unbelieving horror, Tal saw her fall on her side, her eyes
glazing, lips becoming slack.

He fired once more, this time at Tal, but only a click could
be heard. Too many bullets must have been used in dispatch-
ing the nurse. The killer pitched his weapon at Tal's head. Tal
ducked, but not till he guessed it was an S&W .38 that was
being hurled.

He started for the man, ready to take the bastard with his
hands and feeling that anger alone would make it possible and
easy.

He didn't expect two doors to open down the corridor, nor
did he anticipate seeing one nurse and the other man who'd
been here as a Secret Service representative. Both were
wide-eyed and astonished at the sight meeting their eyes.

"It's Talbot Lion," somebody called out.

"And the gun's next to him," the girl shouted. "He's
killed Mickey!"

The actual murderer called out, "Kill the bastard now,
don't wait!" But the genuine Secret Service man was hesitat-
ing.

Tal considered and turned down alternatives in seconds. If
he stayed to argue he'd be able to make his point in time.
After all, the killer's prints were on the gun, not his. But it'd
take time, a lot more of it than he could spare. As soon as the
choices were framed in his mind, one was acted on. Tal
turned and ran, zigzagging out to the entrance. He moved so

quickly that he didn't know if any bullet was fired after him, but didn't think so.

The car was waiting. He jumped in, started it feverishly, and had cleared the grounds by the time he heard another car coming from the same direction.

CHAPTER TEN

"In some ways, I'm a damn sight luckier than I'd have expected," Tal said.

"I wish *I* were," the girl responded.

He meant his words. A while ago he had recollected that Cindy Hatch lived on Vermont Avenue, not a block and a half from the Burlington Hotel, in a three-room apartment. Cindy, whom he had known for years, was a hooker who did most of her business with Washington officials and some congressmen and senators. She had on occasion worked in the Senate Office Building and once, years ago, on the floor of the House of Representatives. Tal had been to bed with her a few times, but at Cindy's bemused insistence no money ever changed hands as a result.

He knew a lot about the attractive brownette, as she called herself. When her father died, she and her mother had moved to Kansas City to live with her Uncle Roscoe and her aunt. Roscoe was attracted to her. She avoided him, but one night when the other women were out, he raped her. Cindy left such scratches on the man that for his own self-respect he threw her out of the house. Cindy was on her own.

She decided to leave town, hitchhiking successfully. In Oklahoma she'd been picked up and sent to a juvenile detention home. There she caught the attention of the bull dikes on the premises. A smart inmate suggested that Cindy sell her services to one of the men who came around to inspect prison conditions periodically, and share the money with other inmates. That would put her in everybody's good graces. Cindy's first experience with prostitution paid off by making her prison time much easier, as she later told Tal.

She ran off to California, hoping to break into movies or television; but a man's promises to get her into a movie

referred only to one of the dirty kind. By the time Cindy
caught on and ankled the premises, several hundred feet had
already been shot. Another man had brought her cross-
country to Washington, where she settled comfortably. Surprisingly prudish in dealing with men, she told Tal that she
hated threesomes or foursomes and judged men by their
manners.

Tal knew he could trust Cindy to keep quiet and had told
her only that he was in trouble and needed a crash pad. Cindy,
of course, had agreed. She never brought men up to her
apartment for what she called "business", and the two of
them would be left alone.

"What are you going to do about your girl friends? I can't
have four in here." She looked annoyed.

"I've never had more than two girls at one time."

"Tal, I meant more than three altogether, and you know
it."

"I've only got one girl now."

"Slipping?"

"Tired of two at a time."

She approved with a nod. "I doubt if your current lady
friend is going to want to crash at my place."

"And I don't think she should, sweetie," Tal agreed.

"I'm sure it's not good enough for her."

"Don't get on your high horse, for God's sake. What I
think is that me and my current lady friend, as you call her,
ought not to be hanging around together. Not for a while."

"Does she know this?"

"She will if you let me use your phone now." He reached
for it at Cindy's gesture, and dialed Renata at the
Georgetown. He doubted if either side of the connection
would be tapped. "Now listen to me and don't interrupt.
Pack your stuff and get out of the Georgetown and go some-
place else. Not the Burlington because it's too close to where
I am. The Raleigh will do it, on Twelfth and Pennsylvania.
You'll be in midtown and that could be a little safer."

"Tal, what have you been up to?"

"I asked you not to interrupt, honey. Don't leave a forwarding address at the Georgetown. Register at the Raleigh under another first name and spell your second a little differently. If you must get in touch with me, you'll have to go through Joe Turk, the information officer at the White House; but don't get into that unless it's a four-star emergency for you. I don't want you to know where I'll be until this business is over and done."

She asked, concerned, "Tal, what happened at Walter Reed today?" In the pause she put in, "There are stories on the newscasts."

"Paint a bigger picture. With more words."

"The stories say that you were present when some false Secret Service man shot a nurse, and you are wanted as a witness."

So it wasn't he who was being accused of murder. Probably because the fingerprints had been identified. He was glad he hadn't filled Cindy in on what had taken place; he might have made it worse and confused the two of them.

"What happened to the killer?"

"He managed to get away."

Damn! "Did they pin a name on the bastard?"

"Not according to the radio or the television."

"Any descriptions given?"

"Not too much, and what there is comes over as very vague."

A good description must have been obtained from any of the nurses or the genuine Secret Service man. There was the suggestion of a cover-up in this.

"What happened," Tal said, "is that the son of a bitching bastard got rattled. He wanted to dust me, but when the nurse started a distraction by saying she'd found out he was phony, he killed her and used up his bullets doing it."

"Tal, you've been very lucky."

"Yes, I was just saying so," he responded dryly.

One good point was that the guard on President Crosby would be made iron-clad after this horror, so that Garth would be safe and the conspirators would have to go around him to start their damn war.

"And you won't tell me where you're staying?"

"Better if I don't."

"Are you with another of your many girls?"

"Renata, it doesn't matter who I'm with. Just relax. You're still number one to ten."

"I don't want eleven having a good time, that's all." Renata sniffed. "Not with you."

"I've got too much on my mind even for that."

"No man ever has too much on his mind even for that!"

"All right, Renata, I'll be in touch or you will. Okay?"

"Wait, Tal, there's something else and it's important. I had a phone call from a man who says he wants to see you soon."

"I'll bet he does."

"He said he's connected with the CIA and knows you."

"Did he give a name?"

"Yes, but I couldn't catch it," Renata said with a stronger accent than usual. "It's very Yankee, if you know what I mean."

"Then I don't see how I could contact him by phone."

"He said that he will be at the entrance to Ursell's at two o'clock this afternoon."

"The department store, you mean?" It must have been suggested because the caller knew that a woman wouldn't forget that message even if she couldn't get names straight.

"Yes, the place with all the Scandinavian merchandise. It's on Q Street and west of Wisconsin Avenue."

"I can find it." On the street, he'd be able to make a quick move away in case of need. "Thanks, honey."

He didn't have anything else to do until half past one but make plans. He decided against carrying a gun to the meeting, even if Cindy could by some damn miracle get hold of one. There might be trouble, and he felt sure he'd have to substitute alertness for a weapon.

The television and radio accounts of what had happened at Walter Reed didn't add much to what he'd been told by Renata. Of course there were reminders of the Kennedy assassination and other horrors, but the media reports showed a distinct lack of hard news.

The business at Walter Reed had isolated him effectively from the President. He didn't have a hope of getting to see Garth or talking to him on the phone. Tal was playing this completely single-o, and didn't like that a damn bit.

The phone rang occasionally while he brooded, but Cindy's answering machine handled calls on the second ring. "Those machines are a big help to a girl in my line," she'd told him more than once, and waited for him to make some nasty remark. He didn't, of course.

Tal paced the small room, stopping only when Cindy asked him to. She was dressing rakishly for the afternoon's "work" and the big night. She could see Tal's eyes reflectively on her in the mirror, and took offense. Tal had forgotten that the hooker felt a constant need to justify herself and her way of life, not realizing that Tal felt entirely uninvolved by her choices.

"Better than being on welfare," she said. "I could probably get welfare if I wanted it. About eighty percent of the clients don't really have any right to welfare. I know an investigator in New York City, and he put me wise."

It was the last subject in the world that Tal wanted to consider at the moment, even briefly. But he was the guest and ought to show courtesy.

"Why doesn't your friend get the chiselers off, then? And all the other investigators do the same thing."

"Because they haven't got the time, none of 'em. I was thinking I'd get a job there, but this fellow put me straight. He said that every investigator handles as many as eighty cases, which makes him responsible for more than a hundred human lives."

"Let the cities hire more investigators, then."

"A city doesn't do that until a unit gets down to one worker or two, it seems. Then the new people need a lot of time to find out what they're doing, so nothing really gets done for a long time and everything goes on like it was. Except that the turnover is high as hell. New people think they're going to do

social work on the job, and then they get their heads handed
to them.''

"I don't see how one guy can handle so many cases.
Doesn't a city like New York think about that?''

"The Department figures that if one investigator can't
handle all the cases on his load, then the thing to do is to hire
an extra supervisor to nag him or her into getting all the cases
done for the week.''

Tal shrugged.

"Anyway, being a sporting girl is a damn sight better than
being an investigator for the welfare. That work is so
demeaning—you know what I mean?''

"Yes, of course,'' he said with a straight face. He looked
affectionately at the brownette, who would have had a fine,
full figure if she could let herself go, whose face would have
been open and honest if that had been possible for her. His
own situation was bad right now, but he never told himself
grim stories about others in hopes of making his situation
look better. "You're right as rain, sweetheart. Right as
rain.''

She had pointed out her stash of coke and grass and good
whiskey in case he was old-fashioned. Tal ignored it all and
took a shower, then made an omelet for himself. At the last
minute he added edam cheese to the mixture, which made it
pleasantly gluey to the taste. There was canned soup as well
and some ham slices along with plastic tomatoes. At least he
wouldn't be going hungry.

With that done, he found a chair for himself and disturbed
the pile of tabloid newspapers, confession magazines, and
romantic novels. By one o'clock he decided that enough time
was being wasted and climbed back into the Volaré.

He expected a problem in getting gas and oil, but the
attendant was completely self-absorbed and impatient—Tal
suspected a girl was waiting for him in the building. Garth
had once told him idly that gas station attendants in the old
days used to be polite, and Tal accepted those words because
Garth Crosby spoke them.

The balance of the drive didn't cause any problems. He wished he could have taken the time to appreciate October in Washington. The air was brisk without being cold. People who had been slowed by the summer's heat were moving around and probably working at their highest capacity. To everybody who heard so much about the pollution and corruption of the environment, a day like this would always be a blessing.

Tal parked in Ursell's lot, as no street space was available. The store, which he observed from the outside, was a heaven of china, glass, stainless steel, furniture, and pottery. Any male customer or passerby would be conspicuous.

He was waiting against the curb on the crowded sidewalk when a man he'd noticed suddenly turned and spoke almost in his ear. "Hell, Lion. What say we go and talk?"

A neutral looking man in good clothes, Tal thought. Probably in his thirties. Clear eyes, small features, a receding chin.

"I asked your girl to send you over and I'm glad she did and you came."

"Miss Waye isn't going to know where I am from now on till further notice, so you or anybody else won't be able to leave a message with her for me."

"I guessed you'd do something like that."

"I just want to get it clear. What's your handle, by the way?"

The man drew out a billfold and pointed out an identification card of the type that Tal knew. Tal's eyes lingered briefly on the name.

"It's Congalton," the well-dressed man said quietly. "Alva Congalton."

"That's what it looks like, sure." Tal spoke absently, trying to remember if he'd heard the name before or seen the man. About the latter, he wasn't sure. He did realize, though, that it was no wonder that Renata hadn't caught that name no matter how often she heard it over the phone when in a state of tension.

Congalton, too, was bemused. "Did Holt really try to slice

you up like so much liver?"

"You wouldn't believe what happened even if I told you."

"I'd heard that he kept swords up at his Watergate *dacha*, but I didn't know he took it seriously enough to try and work you over."

Tal shrugged. He was glad the story was probably known to Washington's best sources, as that would help protect him in case of further trouble. Holt would know he had over-reached, and be more careful from now on. Well, hopefully.

"We'd better cut the air over here," Congalton said, and gestured to the curb. His car was a silver Porsche 79 930, and Tal kept from making remarks about high-paid government jobs. He settled down on part of the red leather interior, glanced up at the sunroof effect, and waited.

Congalton was waiting in turn for Tal to talk. He obliged, but not with words along the line the other was expecting to hear.

"Make your play and I'll get out," Tal said.

"This doesn't make it easy for me, but here goes. You've been working too close to the bull, pal, and there's a warrant out for your arrest. A sealed warrant, so it's not public knowledge yet."

"Did Holt grease the wheels for that?"

"Officially, I don't know anything more."

"What's the charge? You can tell me that much."

"Murder."

"I'm accused of wasting that good looking nurse at Walter Reed, is that it?"

"Yes."

"There are witnesses who'll testify for me. I don't think they can all be bought or swallowed up."

"Well, you might beat the case after a long time, but think of the headlines. Won't do your half-brother any good, those headlines."

Tal sighed. "All right, there's a warrant. It'll be quashed if I do something. What's the price, as if I couldn't guess real good?"

"Keep away from Washington and the President and his

business until Crosby is well enough to leave the hospital.''

Tal didn't know whether the agent was aware of using coded words. The offer was simply that Tal wouldn't be charged with murder if he let the Cuban invasion go through without trying to stop it.

"How much more do you know about any of this?" he asked.

"Not much, and I don't want to," Congalton said. "Anything you tell me is nothing more than gossip or what's known in law as a self-serving declaration.''

Tal considered. Only by giving his word could he get away from Congalton without added violence.

"Okay, I guess that's a deal.''

"Glad to hear it," Congalton said sincerely.

Tal guessed that the man sitting at his side would never be an ally.

"Tell me this much: is the real killer's name known? The man who killed the nurse, I mean, while posing as—''

"It's under control," the other said finally, keeping Tal from saying more. He wouldn't hear details. A man with his expensive tastes wasn't likely to take the chance of finding out enough to put him in any danger of possibly losing this job.

"All right," Tal said, seeing that he'd get no more information from this source. He opened the door. "I just wanted to be sure that the government was being absolutely straight with me, and not stooping to anything like blackmail.''

He walked away before Congalton could say anything in response to that bitter comment.

Tal drove back to Cindy's place, convinced that he needed an ally in this mess. There had to be somebody he could work with.

And standing in front of Cindy's apartment house on Vermont Avenue, no less a ghost from the past, was Crane Rickert.

CHAPTER ELEVEN

"I came up because I knew Cindy would be able to reach you if you were in Washington," Crane said. They were sitting in Cindy's living room, and Crane was wrapping himself around a stinger with Southern Comfort in it instead of the old reliable brandy. "I tried to reach Cindy on the phone, but got the answering service and nothing else but."

"Sorry about that," Tal said.

The two friends had done half an hour's worth of talking. Crane, looking very *cubano*, as he said, told what had happened to him in the last few years since he ducked out of the U.S. to escape the credit mill. He was himself now a strong anti-Communist, and said that the Cuban people weren't so firmly against Fidel as yet, but they were getting there.

Tal spoke about the projected invasion of Cuba, adding only that it had to be stopped and there wasn't much time.

Crane considered. "It'd be a great thing if the damn Russians wouldn't come in, but they'd be in the Sierra Maestre mountains with Fidel before you could say 'Vamos'. Damn them!"

"Don't you think I know they'd be there?" Tal fumed.

"Of course, after their destruction of Afghanistan, I would think that popular sentiment in Russia itself would keep them from another invasion." Crane scratched his unshaven chin. "It's not profitable to the bastards except for vanity."

"I know it isn't, and—" Tal stopped himself. "Well, that's an idea. The first one I've had since puberty, it feels like."

"What are you babbling about?"

"That's easy enough, Crane. If I can't find any powerful helper among our own people to stop this, maybe I can find one among the Russians."

Igor Gurianov, a burly, black-bearded man, was a minor
trade official to the public but covertly a high-ranking captain
in the Soviet Committee for State Security, the *Komitet
Gosudarstvennoi Bezopastnosti*. The major part of his actual
work for the KGB these days consisted of evaluating reams of
material provided by hundreds of different sources. If he was
in luck, he might be able to guide others in piecing together a
picture of some new United States or British weapon. He
dealt with clerks and cryptographers, mathematicians and
military analysts.

In his years in Washington he had been of great help in
giving his masters information about a huge new missile
installation at Orford Ness in Britain. He was also able to
bribe engineers for electronic and computer equipment. He
was one of three men who had stolen a Sidewinder missile
from a supposedly highly guarded NATO source at Zell in
West Germany, and drove three hundred miles along the
autobahn to the city of Krefeld with that nine-and-a-half-foot
rocket sticking out of a window. It was Gurianov who
suggested sending the works to Moscow by air freight, certain that nobody at the German customs office would bother
about the contents. And it was Gurianov who boarded a jet
for Moscow with the Sidewinder ignition switch in his hand
luggage.

He had helped steal a French-built Mirage 111-E fighter
from the Lebanese Air Force. He had bought the plans for a
Phantom-fighter missile and radar system while in Tokyo.
All this had happened in the sixties, and it was often hard for
him to realize that he'd worked for Mother Russia all those
years.

Gurianov was as much at home in KGB headquarters in
Moscow as anywhere else in the world. He'd spend weeks at
the Dzerzinsky Square headquarters, across from a children's
department store and round the corner from a book shop. He
had never ventured below to Lyubyanka Prison, where political prisoners were kept.

Over the years he had become close to the heads of KGB's
chief directorate, and had known Alexander Sakharovsky, its

top man, well enough. In various chores, he had ostensibly worked for the Moscow Narodny Bank, Soviet Export Films, the Russian Lumber Import Co., Aeroflot, Intourist, and Black Sea Baltic Insurance. He'd been attached to other firms, too, but couldn't remember them.

For six months he had worked at the Soviet embassy in Washington, at 1225 Sixteenth Street; that tightly shuttered residence with a mansard roof bristling with antennas. He had been part of the mission to the United Nations until recently. Now he worked for a small firm which did some exporting and less importing; but a big business in state secrets.

He knew Talbot Lion distantly, and had acquired some notion of Lion's services to the American government. Because of their different positions, the two men would never like each other or be close. Lion had once badgered him for half an hour by listing the imperialist aggressions of the Soviet government, and Gurianov had simply walked off.

He was more than slightly surprised to be told by his secretary that Mr. Talbot Lion wanted to see him and that it was important. Gurianov, certain that only a major difficulty would bring Lion out here, nodded for the man to be let in.

As was usual between the two, the preliminaries were short. Lion's first major interest was an assurance that the room wasn't bugged and that their conversation wouldn't be recorded. Gurianov assured him. Lion didn't believe it, but supposed that the Russian might have some bug on his body. He knew that neither preferred to be seen with the other on the streets of Washington.

Tal spoke briefly and to the point. "What you have to do is for your government to tell my government," he finished, "that an attack against Cuba is a declaration of total war against Russia."

Gurianov, considering, leaned forward and disconnected the recording switch that was out of sight. The equipment was new and excellent; a small three-wire tap that could be fitted in seconds to the base of a telephone. Clipped to the proper terminals, it picked up every word spoken in the room when the phone wasn't in use, and words spoken in both directions on the instrument. The three-way would transmit what it heard by radio and worked indefinitely. Another device could translate dialing clicks into telephone numbers that had been called, but it wasn't necessary here.

Gurianov was startled and would have been ashamed of himself if the feeling wasn't so strange. Lion had come here to do him and his government a considerable favor, though for selfish reasons.

"There are wild men in Moscow, too, and they would relish total war."

"I know that, of course."

"But total war must not be," Gurianov added strongly, convinced that Mother Russia would gain her objectives against capitalism one step at a time.

"No, it must not be," Tal Lion agreed gravely.

"I can say pretty definitely that what you suggest will be done," Gurianov nodded, stroking his beard. "A public statement, too, might be of use."

"Certainly."

"We will both be considered cowards in the eyes of some people in our respective governments." Gurianov ruminated. "Is it this—this agitation that lies behind your recent troubles?"

"Yes." Getting to his feet, Tal stopped before turning. A notion had come to him. "If I could get a confession from the man who actually did that murder, I'd be ahead of the game."

"Ah, yes." Lion was obviously asking for a favor, and one which was well within his capacity to offer. The men detested each other but had become allies. "And you think that I would have this information?"

"That's your job, getting information."

Gurianov agreed. It was against all precedent, his offering help to an American who worked against Mother Russia; but different situations certainly needed different responses. Felix Dzerzinsky himself, the first chief of KGB, would have agreed completely.

"His name is Philip Widen." With the help of a file card in the nearest drawer, Gurianov spelled the last name and read the balance of what was written there. "He subleases an apartment at number 408 East 20th Street in New York City. He owns the E-S-E Company, with offices at number 1001 East 180th Street in the Bronx. The firm manufactures furniture. He is divorced and his current girl friend just died. I can guess at whose hand! A fine fellow, this Mr. Widen. His allegiance, as I need hardly tell you, is to the radical conservative cabal in your government."

"Thank you," Tal said bitterly.

Gurianov, no fool, must have noticed that Tal's lips were turned down at the corners.

"Who'd have guessed that I'd ever owe you a favor?" he asked Gurianov.

"It will probably be the last time," Gurianov said pleasantly.

If he had been dealing with almost anybody else, Tal would've said something cheerful and even smilingly made a point of agreeing. He didn't. From the bottom of his heart he detested this man and everything he stood for, completely detested his one powerful ally.

CHAPTER TWELVE

"Don't lie to me," Alva Congalton snapped. "I know you've killed more than one woman and I'm sure I can nail you for that."

Philip Widen felt the blood drain from his cheeks. A darkly self-assured looking man, he regretted having admitted this well-dressed stranger who claimed to work for the detective agency representing him in his divorce. An accusation of having committed one murder would have disturbed anyone, let alone more than one. And no less because it was true.

"You have a lot of protection for what you did in Washington, but what you've done on your own, so to speak, makes you a target," Congalton continued. "So you'll do what I want."

"Get out!" Widen opened the door swiftly.

"Do you want a passersby in the hall to hear and see you being called out for what you did?"

"Move out of here if you don't have a paper to take me in," Widen snapped.

"All right, then, let everybody hear about the murder of two nights ago."

Widen glanced speculatively at the confident stranger's powerful build and closed the door. He didn't lock it. Standing in front of the telephone permitted him to make the point wordlessly that he'd call for assistance in case of need.

"I can prove what you did," the stranger said calmly. "There's positive proof."

"Really? Well, this might almost be comical." Widen didn't look amused. "For one minute, then, but no longer. Impatience has got its limits."

The stranger gave the impression of settling himself for a longer stay.

"Miss Andrea Darrow—" Widen wished his hand had kept from darting up as if to hide him "—was found in her apartment on Avenue A near Eighth Street just two nights ago. She was dead. She'd been murdered."

"There's nothing new in some woman being murdered." Nobody could ever be aware of how much self-control it needed to say those words quietly. "I think I read something about it in the newspapers."

"The papers haven't got everything, I can tell you! Or at least they're not printing it. They write that a window in the murder room was wide open and hint at the notion that somebody broke into the apartment."

"What makes you think it isn't true?"

"The intruder was there for a while, and nobody would leave a window wide open on a chilly October night. Not unless it was supposed to convince the boys at headquarters that the killer came from outside."

"Holmes, you astound me!" Sarcasm wasn't one of Widen's ordinary conversational gambits.

"So we can be sure that the killer is somebody who was let into the apartment."

"An errand boy?"

"None were permitted into the building on that night."

"The janitor, maybe? A doorman wouldn't know what he was up to."

"This janitor's wife keeps a logbook of every repair job and takes the calls asking for her husband's services. There was no entry for Andrea Darrow on that date, and the book hadn't been tampered with. Besides, one look at the janitor and you'd know that there isn't a discriminating woman likely to go for him."

"I noticed his picture in the papers, myself." Widen's tone was almost light. "It could've been the doorman, I suppose. He'd hurry up to the apartment, invent an excuse to be let inside, and hurry down again after the crime."

"It would have taken longer than a few minutes, and the squad car boys who patrol the neighborhood saw him on the job during their irregular patrolling. If they hadn't, they'd have investigated."

"Somebody who lived in the same building did it, then. He just got in and went back to his own apartment."

"She wouldn't have let anybody in if that person lived there. She was standoffish with those people."

"You're ruling out every possibility."

"Except that of her current boyfriend," Congalton pointed out. "Andrea Darrow was never without a man and usually one who was comfortably fixed."

"I didn't know the lady." Instead of being sarcastic this time, Widen was lying with all the earnestness he could call up. "I haven't been officially connected with her."

"That's easy enough to explain. The Darrow woman liked gifts from her men, and usually in the form of jewelry to make her happier. Often the jewels were resold after an affair, but she usually had some pet items around. None were discovered in a search of her rooms."

"You aren't explaining my lack of connection with the woman."

"A little more time, Widen, and I'll get to it. The rooms were ransacked by her killer, and—"

"She may have had a safety deposit vault—no, she didn't," he added involuntarily. "I remember reading that."

"Funny how the details come back," Congalton said idly, and Widen flushed. "Her desk was found wide open, including one so-called secret drawer between two visible ones."

"And it was empty." Widen's voice was thin. "There was a photograph of the scene."

"You took the jewels out so as to make it look like robbery had been the motive."

"Somebody did something, sure." Widen was drinking bourbon-and-branch from the sideboard of this subleased apartment. "I haven't heard explanations or seen proof. And I still haven't seen your warrant."

"Here comes the nitty-gritty. That desk in her room was made by the E-S-E Furniture Company, which you own."

He had expected that. "A lot of people have business with the firm. I've spent a fortune advertising in the women's pages of the papers."

"I wouldn't be surprised if your office records showed a delivery to Miss Darrow."

"I've got many customers." Widen grinned. "And salesmen."

"My point is that you fit the qualifications and you'd know where to find the secret drawer and take back the jewels you'd given her."

"There's no reason to have committed murder. Robbery would have done just as well."

"I'm guessing now, but the Darrow woman had a reputation for polite blackmail, and if you hadn't been generous with gifts she could have promised to testify against you in your wife's divorce action—"

"Another item you saw in the papers, I suppose! About a messy divorce."

"—if some kind of payoff didn't come through. She'd have cost you a fortune. You probably killed her on the spur of the moment and took the jewels to make it look like a robbery."

"Do you have any acceptable proof of this taradiddle? Of course not!"

"Well, the doorman saw a nicely-dressed stranger leaving the building after the murder and might recognize that man again on a line-up. I guess he forgot that you went up with Miss Darrow, and you'd never have gone to her place until that night."

"You've got enough evidence to hang a dozen men," Widen snapped.

"No, it's not—agreed. But possession of the jewels is more than enough evidence."

Widen felt cold. "If I had taken the jewels, I wouldn't have kept them."

"Throwing them away would mean taking a chance that they'd be found and the robbery story would go up in smoke. A vault is out because any search warrant could get to it."

Congalton gestured to a desk like the one in Andrea's room. Formerly it had belonged to Widen's wife and he hadn't got around to having it hauled out of the apartment. "I'll mark up that damn desk till I find the secret compartment with Andrea Darrow's jewelry and then you're done. D-e-a-d, done."

Widen nodded slowly. He had taken his risks, and lost. From a space between the second and third drawers of the desk he pulled out the necklace he had torn off Andrea Darrow's warm body, as well as the additional pieces he had taken to help his story along.

Congalton scooped up the jewelry from the cocktail table and hurled the pieces into a pocket. Widen smiled bitterly.

"You'll be putting on the handcuffs now, I suppose."

"Hell, no!" Congalton shook his head fiercely. "What you're to do is go to an address I'll give you. I plan to wait behind, myself. That address is for what's called a safe house. You'll be outfitted with a new identity and sent to another state to make a new life for yourself."

"Very kind treatment for murderers," Widen said wryly. "Is this a new rehabilitation program, by any chance?"

"No, it's an old program being extended to you because you thought you were doing a job for the government and we don't want that to come out." A downturn of the lips showed Congalton's personal distaste for Widen and for this assignment as well. "Don't take any clothes with you except what you're wearing. Those will be destroyed at the safe house."

"You don't know everything about me," Widen said with another smile, reaching into the closet for a heavy suitcase and pausing at yet another. "One suitcase is vital. As for the other stuff, I'm sure I can get that at the safe house of yours. Or they can send for it if necessary right away."

"Why do you have to take that along?" the Secret Service operative asked.

"You'd be surprised if I told you," the darkly self-assured Widen responded, taking a note that Congalton handed him. "But I can tell you this much right now: my very life depends upon what is inside this suitcase."

CHAPTER THIRTEEN

Tal Lion arrived at the building on New York City's East Twentieth Street by late afternoon. The outer door led to a staircase, and sunlight hurried inside when he opened it. No elevator was in sight.

Crane Rickert, walking at his side, was more used to stairs and led the way up to the sun-flecked first floor. The sound of voices from behind closed doors was an irritation, and the number of languages being spoken was a source of wonder. At a burst of Spanish, Crane smiled tolerantly.

As Tal looked around, a clicking noise could be heard. A door was being unlocked. He would have felt better knowing who was behind it, but didn't.

Crane, having returned to America from a society in which people lived more closely with each other, didn't have any hesitation. He turned to the nearest door and probed it with a hand on the knob, pulling and then pushing. Locked. Before Tal could speak, he was at the next door in the row. Here he wasn't any luckier. As soon as he approached door number three he saw it open.

Alva Congalton, arms akimbo, looked past the startled Rickert to Tal Lion.

"It won't take long, but we've got a few things to talk about," he said to Tal. "There's damn little time, if you want to know something else."

"So you got him tucked neatly away," Tal said even as Congalton stepped aside to let him pass through the door. Crane Rickert, flinching at the presence of a man in authority, nevertheless threw back his shoulders. Congalton shut the door and stood in front of it.

"I knew you'd show up because you had been in touch with Comrade G., and he was sure to give you this address just as you were sure to ask for it," the Secret Service man said quietly.

"I damn well hope you're proud of yourself," Tal said, his voice rising to a snarl.

The room was crowded with furniture. Crane ignored an ivory-painted white fireplace that was mercifully banked and started for the dark sofa. A sudden turn brought him to a high-backed oak chair, which he sat in.

"I'll make it short and sweet," Congalton said. "The warrant against you has been activated, Lion, if only as a way of keeping you quiet for a while." He raised a hand. "Don't give me any details about what you're doing and why. I don't want to know them. I'm following orders, trying to keep a good job. I don't care what sort of political mess you're plumb in the middle of."

"It's not—" Rickert began.

"You shut up, too, *amigo*," Congalton snapped. "Yes, my people know something about you, too. Just keep quiet and let me finish. I'll be getting out of here in a few minutes and leaving you to it. You'll wait. Don't try to leave by the window because a police car is outside and the cops have got orders to shoot."

Tal's lips tightened. "And what's next on your agenda?"

"Two men will be back to take you downtown, and to Washington by private plane. That particular method is cockeyed, but those are my orders." He added bitterly, "And you go for sure without a suitcase."

Seeing Rickert's brows rise, Congalton was moved to add, "That dumb bastard Widen insisted on taking a heavy suitcase with him. Why, I don't know. And it doesn't make the least difference, really."

He turned to the door, then opened and closed it on himself as Tal watched. A lock sounded in the door, then a second lock. Crane was already at the window. As Congalton's footsteps retreated down the hall, Rickett nodded dispiritedly. A police car was on the street, and parked.

Tal made sure that the phone was disconnected and that there was no other exit. The outer door was so strong that two men couldn't batter it down. Worse yet, there'd be no way to get out of the building if they could.

"It's a shame that Fidel's boys didn't teach you how to pick locks," Tal said. "We might get out of here in different clothes and low-brimmed hats, and maybe have a chance."

"You're expecting trouble?"

"Bet your ass I am—now."

"You think that guy has a killer waiting in the wings?"

"Not knowingly. I think his phone call will be processed routinely and it'll be a signal to somebody else who'll come and pick us out. Two hoods, I guess."

"That guy won't stick his paddle in."

"Alva Congalton is a civil servant," Tal said mirthlessly, remembering Cindy's opinions about the breed. "Let's see if we can find anything here that might be of some help. Any port in a storm."

In the kitchen he discovered two small sharp knives and gave one to Crane. He searched the closets without finding anything useful.

"Didn't Congalton mention a heavy suitcase? There might be another, and we can use all the portable weight we can find if only to shove it against the door. Here's another, and it's loaded. But why would anybody keep something inside a suitcase in an apartment?"

Pulling it down from the shelf he opened it to discover various impressive bottles and cannisters. He read two labels, pursed his lips, and whistled soundlessly.

"Comrade Gurianov doesn't know everything," Tal said quietly. "That's a relief."

"What do you mean?"

"This stuff consists of about ten to fifteen pounds of accessories for a dialysis machine."

"A what?"

"I forget you've been out of the country for a while. People who suffer from chronic kidney disease have to be near a dialysis machine that purges the blood of poisonous

wastes which the kidneys can't handle any longer. The blood
is pumped past an artificial membrane and into the purifying
fluid, which is a mixture of water and salts. There used to be
giant machines to do that, but now they've been improved
and compacted. The pumps work faster because they're
smaller, and plastic containers hold the mixture. I understand
that somebody has figured out how to manufacture a wear-
able artificial kidney so that a patient can walk around during
the five hours it takes for the process to be completed.''

"Are you saying that this guy killed a woman and did
whatever else in spite of this—this thing?"

"Got it. I'll tell you something more."

"Like what?"

"Wherever this guy goes, this Widen, we can trace him."

"On account of the kidney machine?"

"Yes, and through the NAPHT," Tal said quietly.
"That's the National Association of Patients on Hemo-
dialysis and Transplantation, I mean. They're on a non-
profit—''

Crane Rickert sighed. "You're not going to trace anybody
to anywhere, *compadre*, except yourself to the grave and me
with you, if what you said about this setup is true."

Tal was already pushing furniture against the door as
Crane Rickert joined him. It seemed like the only possible
protection.

CHAPTER FOURTEEN

The cab turned carefully onto Thirty-eighth Street and First Avenue, on the sight of houses glittering in the late afternoon October sunshine.

Philip Widen, in the back seat of the cab, had never been under so much tension, knowing perfectly well that whatever took place in the next hour would decide his future. He held his hands tightly together in what he himself didn't recognize as unspoken prayer.

The cab stopped in front of a two-story house, and Widen stepped out. He paid and, taking the life-and-death suitcase, stepped out and turned toward it. The door opened on a heavy, nondescript man who stared at him briefly.

"Mr. Widen?" the man asked, approaching. "There's been a slight change in plans, so please follow me."

Widen might have asked for details or confirmation or some proof if he had been in a different frame of mind. As it was, he was still so surprised at having been tagged for Andrea Darrow's murder that he asked no questions and felt no doubts.

"I'll take your suitcase," the man said politely.

"No."

"Well, it's just a short distance so I'm sure you can handle that without any trouble."

There was a half-block to cover. A three-story house was in sight. The man opened the door with a key. From the interior Widen heard a man's drawling, self-assured tones.

The man stood at the far end of a wide hallway. He was perhaps thirty, with sandy hair and drooping eyelids. His face was almost Indian red. He wore a sweater and a necklace of coins to the midriff, jeans and running shoes from the midriff down.

"Go upstairs, please."

"You're Mr. Vale? Pleased to meet you."

There was no response. Widen nodded and took the lead at Vale's abrupt gesture. At a sharp curve in the long staircase, with its sparse portrait paintings, he looked into a cast-iron framed, round mirror and saw a man's frightened features looking back at him.

In the large room to which he was led, Widen took a chair and lay the suitcase carefully down at his side. The messenger who had brought him came in with a tray that held tea and a coffee pot with enameled gray cups, and what looked like small wheatcakes on bonbon dishes. He put them on a deep dark brown wooden table between chair and sofa, then walked to a corner of the room and waited. Vale's voice took on a businesslike tone.

"You have a note for me." He was holding out a hand before Widen nodded.

He passed it across, eyes narrowed. Vale took it between thumb and forefinger and tore the paper in half, then quarters.

"You were assigned to do a necessary job," Vale began, a self-assured smile making the corners of his lips seem even heavier than nature had intended.

"On the President, yes," Widen agreed. "I'm sure he's been badly scared and knows we put a lot of importance on this invasion."

"But you killed somebody else. A nurse, in fact." Over Widen's silence he dashed the possibility that Widen's interpretation of those actions was accepted. "You could've done any number of things. You could've used a medicine ball, which you were offered."

Widen nodded weakly, knowing that Vale was referring to a hollow pellet no larger than a BB shot and filled with deadly poison derived from the castor bean. It was a successful weapon that the Russians had used more than once in Western Europe.

"You could've used electroshock in a hand-carried, battery-powered unit," Vale continued. That weapon, as Widen had been told, projected insulated delivery wires at high velocity to a subject who might have been dozens of feet away, and current was passed through that subject. "But again you refused."

Widen nodded quietly, rather than admit once more that he was scared gutless of the new technology that had been offered to him in working with a government agency. A strong sense of what he considered patriotism was different from using Buck-Rogers type of weaponry to gain necessary objectives.

"We even offered you a chance to use the latest electro-sleep techniques and you refused," Vale reminded him. "Okay, if that's what you wanted. We got you into the President's guard, and you failed. Instead of capitalizing on a resemblance to the agent you replaced, Widen, you instituted a pointless diversion. You bungled the assignment completely."

"I'm sorry. You must know that."

"Sorry isn't good enough," Vale drawled. "Now we have a fresh problem. There's an agent who knows too damn much and who can be made to talk."

"I wouldn't ever—"

"You're vulnerable," Vale pointed out, and looked down at the suitcase with the life-preserving equipment inside it. "Hold that out on you, and you'd talk."

Widen wanted to pick up the suitcase and run out. It was impossible. Indeed, no sooner had he thought of it when the attendant in the room moved forward swiftly and reached for it. Not being strong enough, Widen couldn't stop him.

"I must have that," he heard himself babbling. "I have to be dialyzed, and soon."

"What happens if you don't get around to it?"

"I'll die! Can't you understand that? You must know—"

"Oh, yes." Vale leaned back. "You'll be poisoned and nobody will have lifted a hand against you. It'll be a natural death."

Widen felt himself growing pale. Deprived of his lifesaving unit and without the least freedom of action, he sat back, unable to move. He felt himself growing sicker. It occurred

to him to wonder, even at this moment of despair, what might
have happened to him if the mission had been brought off.
Wouldn't he have been killed in those circumstances also?
He didn't know for sure, and felt as if he didn't want to.

His body was knotting up, his teeth tight together against
their mates, his hands made into fists. He wouldn't let this
bastard Vale get off scot-free. He had killed two times in his
life and would do it again.

He hurled himself forward on unsteady legs. Vale moved
swiftly, a hard sweaty hand thudding against Widen's.

He reeled and knew that nothing more could be done. His
life was finished.

"Take him upstairs," Vale ordered. "I don't want to see
him snuffed out. I'm not a goddam sadist, you know."

The attendant was very close to Widen as he picked himself up, drawing only slightly away but not allowing space
enough for him to run even if he could. These men knew
exactly what they were doing, having taken him away from a
government approved installation to kill him. He had known
from the first that they were part of the government but not
acting officially, had accepted the cut-throat acts and never
dreamed that he himself might soon be the subject of one of
those acts.

He could only walk on unsteady legs up the next flight of
stairs, holding onto the bannisters as if to life itself. Doors to
other rooms were wide open, the rooms themselves empty.

As he was led up to a dark door, a plea formed on Widen's
foaming lips. It was never spoken. The door was locked on
him with a swift click.

This room stank. Others must have been kept prisoner in
this place, too. There was an empty wine bottle on the floor.
The window was well up above his reach. Words had been
scrawled on the wall, graffiti put there by other prisoners.

Widen's throat felt parched and his insides felt as if he had
been drinking paint or something like it. He sank down to the
floor, knowing that he would soon be dead and on the floor of
a dirty room. A natural death, indeed! He wondered if he had
been chosen as a tool in the first place, a living tool, because

his inevitable death could be made to seem natural.

He had never felt more sick. He covered his mouth to keep from calling out, not wanting to give those bastards the satisfaction of hearing him cry with pain. The new life he had hoped for, the chance to be a man of importance, had been denied, cruelly taken away with his existence itself. He had been lured on by men who leered in sympathy, who smirked in agreement with his half-baked ideas, who sniggered their consolations.

He tried to move before remembering he was on the floor and then lay back, dropping a hand. He heard himself speak without knowing the words, and felt he sounded like a child who couldn't keep to a point, couldn't speak with the least care. He was being incontinent as well. His pants were wet and they smelled. He had heard that the bladder emptied after death and not before. In his case, that was wrong.

He called out, unable to help himself now, unable to stop the pain that took over each part of his system. He had known that someday his body would turn traitor and make him fatally sick, but not that it would be so bad. He couldn't seem to stop calling out. Even his hair felt as if somebody had clenched it. There was pain in the most unlikely places.

He started to throw up and emptied his system of recently swallowed food. He lay back, aware that consciousness was going. Finally, he closed his eyes and after only a few more minutes of agony was grateful that in seconds he would know nothing, feel nothing, and be dead.

In seconds he was.

CHAPTER FIFTEEN

"Here come the bastards," Tal Lion said.

"Are you sure?"

"Two sets of footsteps running along the hall, men's steps. You've got your knife?"

"Sure, Tal. What do *you* think?"

Tal didn't answer. The intruders had come to the door. He heard a key in each lock. The men tried to open the door but were stopped by the furniture piled up against it. Tal and Crane stood behind the furniture, pushing back as the killers tried to push forward.

"Son-of-a-bitch," one of the men murmured. And, to the other, "What'll we do?"

"One by the door, one by the window," a deeper-voice replied. "They haven't got hardware, and the cops on guard in the car will know damn well that you're going in and not out."

"Lock this door again and we'll both go the window route," the higher-voiced one said. "Two is better than one."

The steps faded, and Rickert looked uneasily toward the nearest window.

"Let's go into the kitchen and make drinks for 'em," Tal said quietly.

Crane Rickert drew in his breath with a sharp hiss through gritted teeth.

"They'll have to find us," Tal explained. By the time he had snapped the window lock in the living room, Crane was doing the same in the kitchen. Tal, hefting the kitchen knife from his right hand pants pocket, joined him there.

"They'll crash the window in," Rickert said.

"Maybe. More likely they don't want to attract any more attention than necessary."

"So it'll be a standoff and they'll wait us out."

Tal said easily, "There are two of us and two of them. What we've got is—"

They heard a hammering at the door and then the furniture that had been put up against it was being pushed to one side as the men entered. Rickert started to run out to push against the door, but it was too late. Tal kept him in place.

"They're coming for sure," he said quietly.

"Played us for suckers," Rickert responded bitterly.

Tal shook his head. He had considered the possibility and decided on a showdown. Any standoff, as Rickert had pointed out, would use up time. That was one of the commodities Tal didn't think he could spare.

Two men were in the apartment now, the door closed in back of them.

"Leave the crap where it is," the deep-voiced one ordered. "It'll look like they expected trouble."

"What's the sense of that?"

"It won't seem like they were taken by surprise and didn't have a chance."

A clear enough sign that Tal and Rickert would be killed, if these men's plans were carried through.

"I only wish to hell that Secret Serviceman had been ordered to tie the bastards up and nobody worried about marks showing on 'em later on."

It struck Tal that the two men didn't work for the government, not officially. That was a source of some cheer. If those two didn't come out of this, the inquiry wouldn't be pushed in a spirit of vengeance. Good news in a bushel of bad that was growing worse, but good news just the same.

And now to get it over. Tal slurred a foot briefly along the dark kitchen linoleum. Crane looked furiously at him.

In the living room, the high-voiced killer suddenly called out.

"The kitchen!"

"Okay." And, more loudly, "Come on out, you two! It'll be a hell of a lot easier that way for everybody."

Silence. Crane Rickert had made a fist with one hand and was holding his knife in the other. Tal trusted his own knife and common sense.

He was gambling on the size of the kitchen door. It was so narrow that two men side-by-side couldn't possibly come through it. Only one at a time had to appear, and that was enough to ease the odds in his and Crane Rickert's favor. Or at least he damn well hoped so.

It was impossible to hear footsteps coming closer. He waited. There was one pivoting sound as a killer turned and then was in the kitchen door, weapon extended.

He was a burly man with a wide-brimmed hat and dark suit. Tal found his mind working more quickly in that split-second than he had thought possible. It was the weapon that first caught his interest; resembling a gun with something like a telescopic sight over it, squat at the rear and narrow in front. Even as he made his first move he recognized the weapon as a dart-launcher, having had occasion to be offered one himself a year ago on a government mission. He knew that the gun could fire either eight milligrams of cobra venom or a little less of shellfish toxin, depending on what was preferred. Deadly and instantaneous and quiet.

Even in those seconds he knew there was no time. The man's eyes met his, and that was enough. Tal, standing less than three feet away, took aim with his knife for the man's heart. It was a tricky moment, with two lives depending on what he chose to do. With thumb and forefinger near the tip, his life stood or fell on holding his weapon correctly; and even more, depended on the knife's weight and heft, which he had checked out before picking it from the cutlery drawer. Then he hurled it. When the killer saw it in midair Tal had already turned, making a zigzag motion, and ducked.

He heard the man draw in a breath and curse; then saw him lose his balance and stagger. The dart gun was raised almost blindly and there was a trigger click. Then the man staggered back.

There was no time to do anything except be grateful he

himself was alive. He then jumped out the kitchen door hoping for an element of surprise. In that much, he was lucky.

The second man, thin but wiry, also carried a weapon. Desperation gave Tal the strength he might not have had at any other time. He raised a foot and kicked the weapon out of the other man's hand, almost spinning him halfway around in the process because of the added momentum. Tal had hoped for that much. While the other was trying to catch his balance he hurled himself at him using his fists and feet and even his head. The other man fell back, his chin high.

The target was too damn good to miss. Tal balanced himself firmly on the floor, weight distributed evenly between his legs, leaned slightly to the right, and then sent a fist to the man's neck. It traveled beautifully and hit its mark. The man's head rolled back, eyes closing. He lost his balance and struck the floor.

"Help me with him," Tal called back to Rickert. His breath had come so heavily he didn't suppose Crane had heard, so he repeated himself. It changed nothing.

Tal guessed what had happened, and that nothing he could do would be of the slightest assistance. He knew, too, that there was some one-in-a-million chance this bastard might be faking. He and the other had tried fakery before, and this might be another try. He couldn't afford to take a chance.

He looked around for twine and found it, then looped enough around one of the man's wrists and another around one of the sofa legs. He tied the knot firmly. To cut the sailor knot from the twine needed a knife. Tal had no compunction about going over to the dead man and pulling the knife out of his heart. The body twitched and then lay still.

Careful to keep the dark red blood from dripping on him, Tal brought the knife to where the unconscious man lay and cut the twine. Once more he tested the sailor's knot. Satisfied, he wiped prints off the knife and then threw it across the room.

He supposed that a police investigation would find his fingerprints in different places in the apartment, but didn't care. He couldn't take time to go up and down the place with rags and wipe off any possible prints. Furthermore, when the true identity of these men was found, Tal didn't doubt he'd be getting a medal for having performed a public service.

There was no more excuse for putting off what else was necessary, no excuse at all.

He stepped over the dead body, not looking down except to avoid the dark blood puddles on the floor. Crane Rickert lay in the kitchen, arms spread wide. The dart gun's contents had entered below the heart and moved upwards. Crane Rickert's lips were spread wide and fingers apart, as if they had been in pain. His body was almost as rigid as if he'd been dead for hours. Moment of impact to death had occupied no more than ten seconds. Tal knew what product had been used to get such quick results: cobra venom.

"Sorry, Crane," he said quietly. His friend had taken a long journey only to meet death in his native land. "Sorry as hell."

He turned away, deciding against changing his clothes in hopes of bluffing the uniformed police in their patrol car outside. He took a wide-brimmed hat out of the closet, though, and put it on his head. Tugging the brim downward, he started out.

He decided to get out of town quickly without being traced. A hitch-flight to Washington would keep him out of public areas, and it couldn't take long to get one for himself.

A cab took him out to the Butler Aviation Terminal for private planes over at LaGuardia. A number of pretty young college-age girls in skirts were arranging to hitchhike rides for themselves, and he could almost understand why the pilot of a Gulfsteam jet made excuses to his request. He didn't do much better with the pilot of a Mitsubishi twin jet or a Sabreliner. A ground crewman, impressed by Tal's own knowledge of private planes, offered him earplugs and pointed him toward the pilot of a piston-engined Cessna 310. It wasn't one of those sleek corporation jobs flying deadhead, without passengers, or on the way to pick them up. But the pilot was headed for Washington and the plane was certainly in good shape.

Tal set himself for a bumpy ride and got one, in comparison to a jet job. It was like a small car on a highway, and at one point he had the notion he'd be forced to call the 121.5 frequency on radio and tell whoever answered that he'd make a surprise landing himself. He had never missed his own Fornaire this much, and promised himself he wouldn't make the trade-in he had long anticipated. Not for a while yet.

It was three-thirty in the afternoon when the 310 landed at Dulles, and Tal felt a moment's regret at having lost Crane Rickert. It bothered him badly, too, that he'd sent Renata Waye off at a time when he'd have appreciated her presence.

A cab took him to the Burlington, from where he was planning to walk to Cindy's place and his actual destination. A newscast was on. Tal learned that Philip Widen had been found dead in New York City's Gramercy Park, and of natural causes. He also found out that there had been three murders in Widen's apartment. Apparently the second hood must've died of his injuries, which didn't bother a vengeful Tal in the least. Widen, it seemed, was suspected of having committed the three killings. No mention was made of dart guns or government interference, and he supposed he'd never hear one word about the mess. Tal was grateful for that much, too.

It crossed Tal's mind that Philip Widen's death could have been induced and not natural. Somebody might have purposely taken that lifesaving machine from him, and that would be the end of Widen. Not knowing the answer one way or the other, and not needing the information at this point, mulling it over was nothing more than a waste of time.

He resumed listening to the newscast, idly at first. His attention sharpened when the item came through that President Crosby's condition was very much improved. Tal frowned thoughtfully as the cab sped across the city of Washington. . .

CHAPTER SIXTEEN

It took more time than he'd expected to change Cindy's mind. He would never know that his cajolery and flattery as such went for nothing. Only his ability to convey to his girl of the moment that she was the only one he ever wanted made her respond at a time when she hadn't originally wanted to. . .

He admired Cindy's languorous movements along with everything else about her that he could see. She was getting out of bed. Swiftly, she dressed in a simple but perfect cotton dress she had worn on greeting him at the door.

"I have to go," she said quickly. "A whole night's work is ahead and that was just a warm-up."

A whole night's work lay ahead for Tal, too, he had decided. All the same, he made the choice of pretending he had nothing to do but sleep. He wanted her to stay, but accepted the impossibility of it. He dressed slowly after having made love. The straight trousers seemed crinkled, the pinstriped shirt seemed made of air, the tone-on-tone striped tie almost impossible to knot. He hadn't worn a vest. Putting on the socks and sturdy pointed shoes was simple enough, but somehow took as much time as his other bemused efforts put together.

"You okay?" Cindy asked.

"Fine." He glowed. "See you in the morning?"

"Sure, honey, if you're here." She pronounced the endearment slowly. She enjoyed being with a man, being a friend or mistress. Cindy was a man's woman, whose friendship gave the lie to stories about prostitutes only hating their customers or being dikes for their own pleasure. This quick, so long after a good time wasn't what she preferred, either, as the averted eyes and deep slow tones made clear. "Are you going out later? Then can you pick up a container of orange juice on the way back? That is, if you get here before the supermarkets close. There's a package store on the—'' She stopped, having read his face. "This is going to be on business, huh?''

She sounded a little scornful, and he wanted to say that his current business involved trying to keep the United States away from an all-out war.

"Yes, honey, business.'' He smiled. "Sorry you have to go out, too.''

Now she flushed, being sensitive to the implied criticism of her being a hooker.

"The money's good,'' she said, and added, "better than working for the government.''

Tal hadn't intended being even remotely critical, and certainly felt no inclination to start an argument. He said pacifically, "Maybe so.''

"Better than working for the city, too, if you want to know something.''

"Neither of us does that.''

"What you do is a kind of civil service,'' she snapped, more than a little confused. He had forgotten that she took great interest in the drawbacks of other people's vocations, collecting them as if to prove that her own situation was better. "I had a friend once, who was a New York City cop. He told me that cops have to take promotional exams whether they want to or not. Some cops can get by because they've already taken so many tests that they can practically figure out the right answers from guessing the way the examiners' minds will work. And there are a few guys who flunk the test but get promoted anyway on account of they know somebody with pull.''

He wondered if she subscribed to the *Civil Service Leader*, but decided against asking.

"A lot of other cops don't want to take a chance on improving themselves, or they like being at the bottom of the ladder with fewer responsibilities. Do you know how those smart apples do? Well, a guy like that has to take the test and pay the ten buck fee, Tal, or else put in an extra day's work without credit. So he pays the fee, goes to the exam room, and leaves his pages empty. It's always done on every exam and everybody knows that, but it keeps getting done. And I hate that kind of thing, wouldn't want it, because it's—''

"I know." Tal remembered the last talk he'd had with Cindy on this general subject. "It's demeaning."

"Yes, that's what it is, Tal, exactly. It's demeaning." She smiled at the good pupil. "Well, I guess I'd better make tracks."

She glanced back at him. Tal, who wasn't close enough for a kiss or embrace, didn't force it. He smiled genuinely at her, but didn't come closer. She opened the door, looked out at the hallway, and then shut the door in back of her. She walked away softly, as if the hallway floor was a mattress. A good kid, but a hooker and a little crazy as a result, Tal decided. A damn shame!

But Cindy's little lecture on Civil Service had put an idea into Tal's head, and he was going to capitalize on it well before darkness. He had to make three phone calls, using every atom of influence that was open to him. On the fourth call, he had reached a Gettysburg number, and asked Mrs. Congalton to put her husband on the phone. Alva Congalton's voice answered warily.

"You're probably being bugged and I don't know for certain what the story is from here," Tal said. "Let's get together and talk."

"Listen, pal, I'm not going to put my ass in the meat grinder for you or anybody el—pardon, Sally—yes, I know damn well what my job is, dear. But there are limits."

"All I want to do is put the whole business in front of you and then you can do what's right."

"Okay, anything's better than the lectures at home. I'll meet you in downtown Washington. Do you know—''

There was a Marriott Hotel on South Capitol Street, and Tal discovered Congalton waiting for him at a table in the nearest Hot Shoppe.

"Bugging is nothing," Congalton said, after Tal had seated himself and ordered coffee, jam, and toasted English. "I had a friend who was on duty in the U.S. embassy in Moscow on Tschaikovsky Street during the microwave flap back in '76. *That's* scary!"

"The Russians were using antennas to charge up their listening gizmoes and jam our monitoring of their communications," Tal remembered, settling himself down.

"Those microwaves can cause cataracts and raise blood fat levels; cooking human cells if they don't lead to heart attacks and interfere with the workings of pacemakers first," Congalton returned.

"Bastards," Tal said quietly.

"Well, the boys put in metal Venetian blinds later and there was talk about a layer of wire mesh under the floors and papering the walls with metal foil that'd be covered by regular wallpaper. But until anything whatever could get done, my friend was scared out of his wee-wee! Worse than that you aren't likely to find very soon."

"So you don't care about maybe getting bugged at home?"

"It goes with the job," Congalton shrugged, which answered every objection.

Tal waited till both orders were set down. The agent had ordered Veal Parmigiana, and handled the accompanying spaghetti with a surgeon's skill.

"Well, what do you want, Lion?"

"I want you to put your ass in the meat grinder, just like you figured." Tal raised a hand to forestall an immediate objection. "You have a job and you've got to put something on the line to keep your conscience intact. You could get a hero's citation for this; you could get reamed. But if you don't help, you'll be in trouble with yourself forever. And I'll see to it that your wife, your Sally, hears about this. And your kids, if you ever have any and they survive the next few months, will know that their old man was a coward."

Congalton had stopped eating. "There's a word for you, too, pal, and it's not even as pretty as that."

Tal ignored the provocation. "You've heard something about what I'm up to and why. What you've heard is biased, one-sided; but I'm sure you've got the idea."

"I never listen to interoffice gossip," Congalton said, the image of a good bureaucrat.

"Do you want me to say out loud what's up in certain important areas of the government? Do you?"

"No."

Tal glanced around briefly. "Better eat up and don't look so upset, or you might draw attention."

Congalton didn't need a second warning. He resumed eating methodically.

"There's nobody else I can go to, and you have to put it on the line," Tal said. "Nobody I can go to for what you can offer, I mean. Damned if I'll talk to you about patriotism, because that's out of style right now. But this country has got a good thing going, and some of us have to take risks to preserve it for our families and ourselves, too. When it's necessary to take risks, of course."

"I want to keep my job, that's what I want."

"Sure, and there's some chance you won't have that or your life, either. We might win our point and you'll be eased out of the agency right afterwards. But you think there's a choice, and I'm sure there isn't."

"Why can't I put the cuffs on you right now and forget the whole business?"

"It might not be so easy."

"I can give it the old high school try."

"Sure, Congalton, but one way is right and the other is wrong, and we've got to a point where even a good civil servant, a bureaucrat who always covers himself, has to stand up and be counted. You know what Garth Crosby stands for, and if he's forced into an all-out—"

"Don't for God's sake!" Congalton looked swiftly around. Satisfied that no one else was in earshot, he sat back and drew a deep breath. Then he nodded. He did it slowly and not willingly, but his nod was enough to put the lie to any theory that Cindy had ever held about people who worked for a branch of government. The decision had been made.

As Tal watched, Congalton reached into a breast pocket for an inch-and-a-half-square rubber pad. From a jacket pocket he drew out what looked like a wallet. A wire attached the pad to an imitation wallet. With two abrupt gestures he disconnected the recording instrument.

"I might've known it's useless to cover my ass with the likes of you around, Lion." He shrugged. "There isn't anybody who can hear us directly, but talk around it all the same. Tell me indirectly what you want."

"The first thing is for you to get a white jacket and wear it," Tal said. "A simple one."

Congalton looked more puzzled than annoyed. As a man who liked to dress well, though, he probably didn't anticipate wearing goods that weren't first-rate.

"Is that all?"

"No, you'll meet me in an hour at this place," and Tal drew a piece of paper off a pocket pad to write down the exact location. He destroyed the three blank sheets of paper under it in case they had retained an impression. Then he himself was taken in hand by somebody else over the next minutes. A considerable time in Washington was given over to covering tracks, making sure of not being followed, preserving the sort of seeming privacy that Americans in years past simply took for granted. Probably little kids in this town did it, too, on their way to meet friends of the same age.

Congalton's eyes had approved of Tal's precaution, but they narrowed as he looked down at the square of paper beside his plate.

"Are you sure you know what you're doing?"

"No—how could I be sure, in this setup? But I don't see any choice, either. And if you stop and think for a minute, you'll see things just the very same way."

Congalton shrugged. "I can bring over a couple of boys who are absolutely trustworthy."

"We could use 'em, God knows, but there isn't any way of being sure *what* they are. In your case—well, I'm almost sure."

"Thanks a bunch."

"Oh, one thing more," Tal added as he was getting to his feet. "See if you can pick up a stethoscope and wear that around your neck. It'll make you look more convincing at a distance, anyhow, and get you inside at the very least."

And he was gone before Congalton's eyes widened in a flash of surprise.

CHAPTER SEVENTEEN

Renata Waye had registered at the Raleigh Hotel as Bonita Way, making a slight difference in her name as Tal had suggested. She was hoping to hear from him soon, and not enjoying the passage of time.

Of course there had been some consolation. Over a solitary late lunch she had caught the interest of a hard-looking, bearded man who came over to talk with her. Having been raised in Europe with different ideas of propriety, Renata was a little surprised.

"Don't worry about appearances, Renata Waye," the man said. He had introduced himself as Sidney Venters and knew of her portrait work. "I can tell you that there are chaperones here after a fashion."

"The waiters?" She almost smiled. "They are deeply involved, to be sure."

"I was talking about—" He turned his head to the right and spoke with another. "The two of you haven't met."

Renata's eyes followed hurriedly. A woman sat at the next table, hand partly raised over her face as if she didn't want to look at anyone else.

"I want you to be very polite to Miss Waye, my dear, as I hope she'll be painting my portrait."

Only then did the woman's eyes slowly meet Renata's.

Venters was telling her, "A chaperone, as I say." He spoke exactly as if no tension existed between himself and the women. "This is my wife."

Before half an hour had gone by, Renata could see that Elsie Venters was terrified of her husband's displeasure. It showed in the way she would widen her eyes and turn to him before speaking, in words spoken quickly when it seemed that he might become irritable. Nothing else explained why

the woman ignored those lustful stares that Venters was
giving the tired Renata.

Elsie was a plain woman dressed to the nines, but her dress
was the wrong color for her pallid skin and its gold buttons
much too bright. Her eyebrows had been blackened conscien-
tiously, but they gave the face a ghostly shade. She spoke in a
lively way at least, but only when the subject had turned to
her children. At one point the children themselves came into
the restaurant to join their elders for dessert.

Renata, as it happened, liked both children at first sight.
Thomas was a tall five-year-old with an almost military
posture. Irma was also tall and only four years old. She wore
a plain dark dress well and her features resembled her
father's. Toward her mother the child showed almost an
indifference. Mrs. Venters, in turn, showed pleasure only in
talking with Thomas. As Renata demonstrated her liking for
the children, however, she was glad to see a warm response
between them and their mother. Venters flashed a wicked
grin at the sight, not realizing that Renata would have cheerfully painted the youngsters but not their father. He wasn't a
very perceptive man.

She took a walk afterwards, but only for a couple of
blocks. Returning to the hotel, she made sure no messages
had been left for her. Then she settled back on the soft chair in
the lobby, wishing she and Tal were back at Cape Ankh in
Turkey and busily engaged in the underwater archaeology
which Tal enjoyed and she tolerated as a setting for various
portraits. She went up to the simple room, which caught the
sun's full tilt. Here she did some sketching, mostly of the
Venters children's faces from memory.

All four of the Venters were eating in the comfortable
dining room over dinner. The daughter ran over and so did
the boy, and when Renata had finished her light meal she
went back with them to the table. At a pointed look from Mr.
Venters, his wife suggested that Renata might want to paint
him. At another signal, she and the children got up and left,
on the way to see friends. Mr. Venters said he'd see them
later, then settled back to speak with Renata. It had all been

well and dutifully arranged for this talk.

"If you'll excuse me," she began.

"Someday I'll be better known than just as a defense equipment salesman," Venters said, disregarding her wish. "My portrait will have a certain value, then, over and above being your work. As Mrs. Venters and I have a house in Atlanta, a beautiful city if there ever was one, you could stay over long enough to do the job and see the city."

"I would rather not," Renata acknowledged, thinking she'd leave her address with Tal if it all didn't involve painting this lecher.

"You can protect yourself from me as long as you want to."

"I cannot count on the closeness of the children for every minute of the day or night, if I paint you at your home."

"Other people are active on the premises during the day, enough of them to prevent anything but an occasional leer on my part."

Mr. Venters seemed bright enough to find a way out of that difficulty.

"Let me make a suggestion for a compromise, my dear. I am willing to bide my time before making a big try. By that time, you'll know me better and feel differently."

He may have realized that her thin smile was skeptical.

"Besides, for a few weeks I'll have somebody else on the string."

"You're a very fortunate man." She made a small gesture by which she meant to indicate distaste for him.

Venters only understood that he had roused emotion in her. "Interested, aren't you?" he asked. "Well, that's more than half the battle between two adults."

"Now you must excuse me," she said promptly, forsaking the training of a lifetime to leave without polite permission from another.

She went up to her room and settled herself in bed. It was early, but she had nothing else to do, and most television bored her unspeakably.

Renata had fallen back gratefully on the narrow bed and

was closing her eyes when she heard the soft unmistakable sound of a key in the lock. For the moment she could do nothing, not even wonder who Venters had bribed to get it. (She didn't know that the defense equipment salesman carried a ring of skeleton keys for demonstration purposes, and that if one didn't work another would.) She had forgotten to put the chain across the door. The sound of the key and the knowledge of what it must mean caused her to force a moist palm over her mouth. Pretending to be asleep, as she had to do for safety's sake, she waited in helplessness and mounting terror.

Not far away, another sound came clearly; a child calling out, a little girl crying because of freshly roused fears of the night. The sound filled this dark room in almost as terrifying a way as the intrusion. If it happened to be one of his own children crying, Venters didn't care.

"You're faking because nobody goes to sleep this early," he said, closing the door in back of him and snapping on the light. "I know you're interested because you as good as told me so downstairs."

She cursed him silently for his vanity and stupidity for not realizing that she had only shown her dislike of him.

"Get out of here!"

"Don't worry, baby, the wife and kids haven't come back yet." He approached slowly, as if to build her anticipation.

"I'll scream! These walls aren't soundproof and —"

"You'll scream with pleasure, baby, I guarantee that. Besides, doing it with a married man under the same roof as his wife is supposed to make it more exciting. That's what I've heard from plenty of girls, and I believe it." He smiled cruelly. "I've waited long enough and I won't be disappointed, now."

At that moment two things happened, and each was in Renata's favor.

The phone rang.

Renata reached out for it instantly, before Venters could make a move to stop her and keep her from speaking into it.

"Tal here," Tal Lion's voice said instantly over hers. "I need your help and it's damned important."

She needed his help, as well. It took only moments for her to decide on impressing this fool in the same room by knowledge of her contacts, and hope to stop his projected assault on her in that way. Perhaps it wasn't necessary. A man who made a living out of the sale of defense materials to the government would do nothing to bankrupt himself, no matter how worked up he had become. And he had stopped in mid-motion, ears cocked.

"Tell me where to meet you and no more," she said sharply.

"Think you're bugged, too?" Tal sounded amused.

"Yes. In a way."

He was too self-absorbed for questioning that. "What I want from you is risky as hell, Renata, and you can say no any time you want to and twice on Sunday—that is, if you don't want to do it. But you can't chicken out if you agree that all systems are go."

"I'll help you, whatever it is." Anything was better than exposing herself to the likes of this fool standing indecisively in the room.

"Okay. I'm going to give you one piece of instruction right now." He considered. "Get to a public phone booth and call ST3-3535. That's the Convention and Visitors Bureau number, but when you ask for me by name you'll be put through on a special line. Have you got that?"

"Yes, of course."

Venters had already turned his back to her and was walking out. Renata broke the connection, locked her door and put the chain across it, then dressed herself and went downstairs. The bearded ruffian was nowhere in sight. She called the number, asked for Tal, and was put through.

"I'll be in front of your hotel in ten minutes, Renata," he said, not waiting for her to identify herself. "Let me tell you once more that the stint is necessary, but it could be damned dangerous."

She was going to say that a visit to Washington was filled with danger in many other ways. Like New York, it was not a city in which to grow old. She sensed, of course, that he was in no mood for idle conversation.

"I'll be there."

"Good girl. Oh, by the way, don't wear too much makeup."

The last words bothered her without knowing why. She decided that she was sufficiently made up and waited in the foyer of the hotel, then stepped outside after eight minutes had passed. It was darker out here, but still safe.

Tal pulled up in a Mercedes 280, a blue car with a white and blue interior. She noticed quickly that he looked tired but determined.

"Hop in and let's move," he said grimly. "We'll stop off when we have to."

"What does that mean? Are you expecting trouble on the road?"

"You mean like those boxes on Interstate 75 in Florida and in Massachusetts, too?" Briefly distracted, he smiled. "Those motorist aid call boxes are on the roads and between cities, as a rule. Easy to keep a contraption like that on a signpost. You simply pull down the lever that covers it and that winds up a small generator inside the box that shows a panel with buttons labeled in English and Spanish for service, Police, or medical needs. And I remember seeing a cancel button, too. Inside is a solid state FM radio transmitter that sends a signal to highway patrol headquarters. One hell of a clever idea, and I wish there were more of them up and down these highways."

Not for the first time, Renata had occasion to fume at the masculine fascination with gadgets. "Can we return to our muttons? What is it that you require me to do?"

For an answer, he pulled up at a darkened section of the city. From the floor at his left he brought up a package. Inside was a nurse's uniform, complete with cap, stockings, and shoes. She looked surprised.

"We're going over to the Walter Reed General Hospital, and you'll help me and somebody else."

"Help you do what?"

"To do the job we can't trust anybody else to help us with, honey," said Talbot Lion. "We're going to kidnap the President of the United States and get him out to where he'll be absolutely safe."

CHAPTER EIGHTEEN

Shortly before reaching Whittier Street, Tal became aware of a Cadillac Coup deVille on the road. Its horn was sounding in rhythm: three short, three long, three short. The SOS signal was sure to attract his attention, and he pulled over. The burgundy colored car drew closer and a man in shirt, tie, and dark pants got out. He carried a stethoscope and white jacket in one hard hand.

"What the hell?" Tal asked.

"I didn't realize it myself until just a while ago, but this'll come off better if you're the one who plays doctor." Congalton flashed an appreciative glance over at Renata, drawing no reaction at all. "The guards know me and I can fake 'em out so nobody will try anything if I'm outside the room."

Tal had figured originally that Congalton's strength would be best applied helping the wounded President get dressed. There was something to what Congalton said, though, by way of objection. Tal didn't think Congalton was a triple-crossing heel ready to sell him out, only a time-server in the best or worst civil service tradition. It was true, too, that the President was most likely to trust Tal and offer the least trouble. Tal hadn't been thinking too clearly when he had decided on the details of this job.

"Okay," he said, reaching for the jacket. Not a perfect fit, but aligning the stethoscope over his neck would help hide the defects. "You're all set now?"

"Right."

Tal's eyes took in the gun in its holster under Congalton's left arm. He nodded. Briefly he made introductions, and Renata was aware of another appreciative glance.

"Renata and I will be going in," he said, "and you'll be outside ready to help in case we need you."

"That's the new deal." Congalton must have caught an edge in Tal's voice because he said quietly, "I'm on the right side. I hate it, but I'm on the right side."

Tal was so taken back he couldn't express his feelings. He said brusquely, "Well, let's haul ass and get the job done."

"Amen to that," said Congalton, and disappeared into his car.

Getting inside the Administration Building posed no problem at all this late at night, especially with Tal's and Renata's uniforms. Congalton, out of sight, had arrived earlier. Tal would have expected somebody to check them out, but it didn't happen.

He found himself with Renata on the way to the President's room. Somebody called out, but Congalton's voice rose above that and Tal was able to walk inside. Renata followed.

Garth Crosby was in a suspiciously deep sleep. Tal called his half brother's name twice, then approached the bed and opened an eyelid with thumb and forefinger.

"Drugged?" Renata asked, although she knew the answer.

"Get busy!" was his only response, going to the closet for Crosby's clothes.

She helped sit Crosby up. After Tal had put on Garth's underwear and pants, careful about the chest bandage, she put on the stockings and shoes. The touch of a female hand caused Crosby to stir. (Renata found herself thinking that even a man who was half-dead could be roused quickly.)

It took less time than she or Tal had expected, and turned out to be easier than he believed possible. For Renata, who had dressed babies on occasion, the work was simple.

"Now comes the hard part," Tal said briskly, straightening. "I'll haul him; you lead the way out to the car. And do it quickly."

The door was opened by somebody else, from the other

side. It wasn't Congalton. The white jackets and alarmed features identified the two men as genuine doctors. They strode in and shut the door, belligerent at this challenge in their domain.

"Damn it, the patient can't be disturbed! He's fallen asleep, you can certainly see that."

"He's spacey," Tal snapped. "Is that what you do when you've got a patient who might see what's happening around him or still able to function? You fill him with drugs?"

Renata added, "And you lie about it."

"Where are you taking him?" one of the men asked. "By whose authority?"

"We're taking him to where his enemies won't drug him. As for the authority—"

The other doctor advanced to the bellpull.

Tal ordered, "Keep away from that." He drew out a blued steel short Colt .38. "Touch that thing and you'll see if I mean to use this or not."

The two men reluctantly did what they were told. Renata stepped to one side.

Tal said, "Now you guys turn around and walk out side-by-side. Do it if you know what's good for you."

"But we'll be stopped!"

"Tell whoever stops us that he's being taken for some tests he has to be walked to," Tal snapped. "Give them a song-and-dance, full of medical terms. Never mind that he's dressed. If you pack enough authority in what you say, it'll be okay. If anything goes wrong, you clowns catch it first."

Tal watched the door open. He and Renata moved slowly with their burden. Tal had to keep his attention on the two shaky doctors as well as the drugged chief executive.

Somewhere in the hall, a buzz of talk stopped.

"What in hell is this?" an unfamiliar voice suddenly asked, raised worriedly.

"Shut up." Alva Congalton spoke very clearly. "Keep your damn hands on the ceiling and shut the hell up!"

"Hey, Al, for God's sake, you can't get away with this,

you and them others!''

"Maybe not, but we sure as hell are going to try—now shut up! Not another damn word.''

In silence, the two doctors walked down the hall with Renata, Tal, and their burden. At the White House Oval Office Garth Crosby would be safe from any possible attempt at doing him harm, and there he couldn't be drugged against his will without it being known to dozens of people on his staff. In the President's case, certainly, he would be safer outside the hospital, and Tal had realized it as soon as the President's condition had officially improved.

The walk was long and agonizingly slow. He managed to give the car keys to Renata, who opened the door to the driver's seat. It took care and thought and muscle to get the sleeping President inside. He murmured once.

Renata had left the keys in the car door, and Tal took them out before easing the President further along to the passenger seat.

"Go around to the other side," he ordered Renata.

She nodded and unknowingly moved into danger.

Tal never saw exactly what happened, but did catch a glimpse of it while adjusting the driver's mirror. He saw Renata move into the road, saw a car suddenly stop near her, then heard Renata shout. And at that moment she was push-hauled into the car, her hands flailing in vain, her feet kicking out. It was useless. Renata was a prisoner.

Tal, in his way, was imprisoned, too. In this of all situations, with the drugged President of the United States next to him, it was impossible to venture out and save Renata from whatever might befall her. He couldn't risk Garth Crosby's life to do it.

As the other car sped off, Tal recognized it as a Porsche Targa, but was unable to see the license number. It had been artfully smudged with dirt so that not every figure could be made out. The bastards in there had taken every possible precaution.

Tal decided he had already used up too much time. Swiftly

he put the Mercedes into a U-turn and started down the roadway. He was trying his best not to feel, not to think, only to be a good and efficient machine himself.

He almost carried it off.

CHAPTER NINETEEN

Renata had seen a man's hands in motion before she felt them, astonished in spite of everything that such violence was happening. One hard hand was planted across her mouth, the other at her back. In anguish she looked from right to left, hoping that Tal would help, but knowing perfectly well at the same time why he couldn't. It would have meant everything to her, but good luck didn't come to those who took risks of this nature. A wild hope crossed her mind: it might be possible to attract attention from a passerby while she was in the car; but she found herself forced into the back, and one of the men kept a foot on her to be sure she stayed on the floor.

Looking up in terror as the car started, she saw the familiar and hateful features of the man she knew as Venters.

"Surprised, aren't you?"

"But you know what I told you—"

"I'm not trying to get you to draw my picture, you damned idiot," he growled. "Now shut up."

She couldn't do that. She understood that at least two men had been involved in this attempt, but nothing else.

"But why—what do you want?"

"Can't keep quiet, huh? All right, I'll tell you the straight poop if that'll stop you from squirming around. I sell so-called defense equipment to the government and I want to sell yay more. The best way is for the country to get into war."

"But that's—that's insane."

"Is a profit-and-loss statement insane? Is a stock quote insane? To hell with that!" He considered. "And look at it assbackwards. Sooner or later we're *going* to get into a war

133

with the Commies. Best to have it over with, while we've got the major advantages, and not them. Don't tell me we aren't doing every American a big fat favor.''

" 'We'. There are other in it besides you and the driver, I assume.''

"Sure." He nodded. "We know about Lion and you, and what sort of jobs Talbot Lion takes on for the President. Soon as you separated from him, I went to the hotel with my wife and kids—''

"They really are your wife and children?''

"Right. I think a family ought to help out the breadwinner when it's necessary; and they gave me a great cover. When I wasn't following you, Skeezix was. The driver. Not his real name, and Venters isn't mine.''

"Why did you come to my room earlier tonight?''

"Oh, that. Figured I could score—still may, if I get the time. Wanted to scare you, though, into calling Talbot Lion for protection so I could get his number and know where to reach him.'' The man called Venters chuckled. "Turned out I didn't have to.''

"What are you going to do now that you've kidnapped me?''

"Call Lion at the number he gave you. Let him know I've got you, and he'd better step aside and out of government affairs if he wants to see you again.''

Renata couldn't imagine Tal changing his course of action as a result of telephoned threats, and was surprised that Venters considered it a possibility.

She shuddered strongly. "You must have a wonderful conscience.''

"You have to know where the advantages are,'' Venters said, talking to keep her still while she hoped to hear something of importance. "Not like the old days at the University of California,'' he chuckled, purposely changing the subject. "I dropped out and lived on campus without being a student. With the help of a pal's registration card I could use the student union lounge, go to class lectures, get free medical treatments and see movies for free, too. I could eat on the

Terrace, meet girls on the Lower Plaza. I went on the avenue, prowling up and down Telegraph Avenue and the self-service laundries—great place to meet girls, in those days—and raise holy hell without ever being part of the establishment. But that was then and this is—Here we are.''

She said, "I will walk where you want me to, but please don't touch me.''

"Sure I can take your word for that, baby." His indeterminate-color beard bristled. "The hell I do!''

As she stood, one of his hard sweaty palms closed her mouth tautly, and his body was less than half a dozen inches from hers. Renata raised both hands and raked her nails across Venters' ruddy cheeks. He swore and struck her contemptuously and with force against the right temple, causing her head to swim. What she had tried to do would never be enough to stop this powerful man determined to have his own way.

His arms were around her midriff to keep her helpless. She moved because she had to, following the driver to an old three-story house in a section of the city she was sure she had never seen. They walked up a flight of stairs, Venters giving her slightly more room. The driver, whose face she hadn't noticed closely, opened the door. She was hurled inside and cursed at. No one would ever be able to guess or sense the terrors she had known in the last few minutes and felt more strongly now.

There was a pause and then Venters pushed her into another room that was almost bare of furniture. She sensed what was on his mind now, fingers clustered in two wide half-circles. Her blood tingled. She would kill him if he tried to do what he was thinking, she knew that much. She would kill him.

He said, "You really hate me, don't you? I've got a good mind to break your hands, so that no matter what else happens you'll never be able to raise a paint brush again as long as you live.''

Renata gasped this time. She hadn't seriously imagined such cruelty from anyone, not such cruelty to her.

No matter what might have been on his mind, he did nothing just then. A knock had sounded on the outer door. He closed the door behind him and went to answer the other. Renata peered out through the crack in the door and could make out part of his movements. She saw the door open and had a brief glimpse of the man who was let inside. He wasn't the driver, but a sandy-haired, red-faced man with drooping eyelids. She was surprised how much it was possible to see through the closed door and then guessed that in the shabby apartment nothing worked well; the door had been planed more than strictly necessary at one time; and no substitute had ever been put up.

Because of it, too, she was able to hear their steps. They entered a nearby room. Having spoken politely for a minute, the two were soon head-to-head in argument.

"Stupidest damn thing I ever heard of," the visitor growled, his words coming clearly. "You let this girl see you and keep sticking yourself in front of her. If you have the hots for a broad who makes it with influential people, get the hots on your own time. I can introduce you to Edward Holt's wife, who I hear is as much of a swinger as he is."

"I figure to put the boots to Talbot Lion by—"

"Oh, sure, he'll give up everything because one girl is threatened," the stranger sneered. "You'll probably spend so much time bragging that you've made it with his girl you'll get no further. Besides, it's all useless. It's your glands that are moving, not your head."

"You've got this all wrong!"

"Not me. Look, I've got no objections to killing, when it's necessary. I saw to it that the guy, Widen, was knocked off by taking away that damn kidney machine of his. So I've got plenty of stomach, you know?"

Renata would have gasped her dismay once again, but forced herself to keep quiet.

"I've done other things, too, in my time; and I think you've got some notion what they are."

"Yes," and the man she knew as Venters paused significantly. Whatever the intruder had done, recollection probably horrified even him. Judging by what she'd just heard, Renata could understand that.

"Now if you want to make it with this broad, wait a while. Don't waste my time now, or yours. Every second counts because if we swing into action you've got to be in top shape for the final push. If everything works out, you'll make your fortune and mine in a few days, enough for life. Is that clear?"

"Yes. I'm sorry. I didn't mean—" Venters paused. "I'll have to kill her after all."

"Just keep her in this place until we get the word one way or another and that Big Three is on." He was referring with those words to World War Three, of course. "Then do what you want with her, whatever that is—as if I couldn't guess." He hesitated. "Good looking?"

"Great."

"Well, you can get her as a present from me. Think of it as a bonus for work well done. But not until this business is settled."

There was talk about what Venters had seen on the path in front of Walter Reed, and it seemed that the man had been so self-absorbed by his quarry he hadn't recognized the President, either. The newcomer was vaguely irritated, and directed Venters to answer the next knock at the door.

It opened to a small man with huge hands. From the first words, she knew him to have been the driver of the car in which she had been kidnapped.

"I was just watching the late television and they put on a news bulletin," the man said, adding that the President had been spirited out of Walter Reed General Hospital and was now entering the White House. Venters cursed. The second man to have come in, the man superior in position to Venters, spoke thoughtfully.

"It's him or us," he said quietly. "The battle for America's future has been, as the saying goes, joined."

Venters sounded worried. "What do you think he'll do?"

"If I were Crosby, I'd probably have every one of us knocked off, from Ed Holt on down. Or at least try and do that."

"But he can't pull *that* off—can he?"

"Well, I can say this much," the superior considered. "I hope to hell that you're right."

CHAPTER TWENTY

Talbot Lion and the drugged President pulled up before the White House. A uniformed and helmeted guard started over to make an inquiry, then halted in his tracks.

"Get a wheelchair," Tal ordered. "I'll take him through."

"But I'm not sure I can—"

"I'll cover your ass and write an authorization myself," Tal snapped. "Now get on the stick!"

A wheelchair was brought out. The President was lifted onto it and wheeled into the house and through the East Wing, past the library, the gold room, the China room, and the diplomatic reception area. Tal took him past the lobby reception in the West Wing's executive quarters, the Roosevelt Room, out to the hallway, then past the study, and into the Oval Office.

By this time the President was almost revived. His eyes were open. He asked for water, which Tal brought. The lights were flicked on in the room, with its Peale portrait of Washington, the gold curtains, round desk, and dark leather chairs. The walls were off-white, a rug pale yellow, and the furnishings in golds and greens and salmons. Renata would have had something favorable to say about the color scheme, Tal thought, and then winced. He didn't want to think of Renata at this time.

Alva Congalton, his face crinkled with worry, appeared in the room within minutes. He'd had very little trouble getting in, as he said dryly, because he was known in the territory.

"The news is on radio, sir," he said to the President. "A print reporter was at the scene, and he got the story to his paper and the radio people at the same time. There was no direct TV coverage because no setback was expected, and networks have been scalded for keeping their cameras around a government installation like Walter Reed.''

"All right," Crosby said. He asked Congalton for his name, which was familiar when it had been repeated. "Get Doctor Mellors in here."

"Yes, sir. I'll use the reception area to make that call."

"And call my wife, too. Put her through to me. Tal, stay planted. Nothing intimate is going to be said on the phone."

He was capable of making a bad joke, so at least he was recovering. "I'm all right, Loretta," he said on the phone, picking up at the signal. "I know exactly what I'm doing and why—No, there isn't any need for you to come down and see me. I have a lot to get done quickly and might be here for some hours yet. Go to sleep and dream about me, darling, that's a good girl—Well, yes. Yes, but it's perfectly all right. No, I won't let myself be talked into anything bad. Word of honor."

He hung up, bemused, and glanced at his half brother. "Loretta is certain that you're responsible for everything and that you're leading me down the road to destruction. She never will trust you even a little, Tal, while you're still single."

"Too bad."

"Well, I've had fewer women by far, but I've had the pleasure of making it in the White House, and *there* is an aphrodisiac, if you want to know something. Well, let's get to business. First item on the agenda is to find out what condition I'm in."

Doctor Mellors arrived in five minutes, black bag in one hand. He and Garth were friends from Illinois; and Mellors, a small, peppery man in his fifties, spoke accordingly.

"Running out of a hospital is a damn dumb thing to have done," he grumbled. "Especially out of one of the world's great hospitals, which Reed is."

"I was being drugged when it wasn't necessary, and I have to know what I'm doing as much of the time as possible. Tal knew I was recovering and saw me drugged."

"That wasn't done on my orders, so maybe some instructions got mixed up," Mellors conceded. "You might be better off here from now on because it's a bodyguard's native ground, and he won't be stymied by somebody who might not wish you well but has got a convincing medical story. I think it's very unlikely myself, but there's maybe one chance in three million."

"What I really needed was a drink, and I'd take one now if it wasn't so early," the President said while being swiftly examined.

"I guess you can have a drink if you want to," Mellors said, having concluded. "Instead of drugs."

The President smiled and paraphrased unexpectedly, "Malt does more than Milltown can, to justify God's ways to man. "Never mind that, Vic. Its just a smart-ass intellectual joke."

"You're in okay shape," Mellors concluded. "But I wish you could spend a couple of days in bed."

"I'll have a cot put into my study and stay there when I get tired."

"All right, and I'll see you again at noon, just to make sure everything's okay."

"Terrific," the President said a little weakly. He glanced at Tal. "That fellow who was here—King Kong, or whatever his name is—can we trust him?"

"It seems that way."

"Right. Do me a favor, Vic, and ask him to come in."

Mellors accepted his dismissal. Alva Congalton was in the room shortly, reporting that the reception and phone area were now almost fully staffed. It was nearly dawn, and a new day was beginning.

"Okay, Tal," the President said, turning to his half brother. "Let's have it now. It's more than time to get our socks pulled up on this."

"What do you mean?"

"I think I understand why you got me out of there, but not why you didn't go to Vic Mellors with your complaints and have him take care of it. There'd have been no flak with the media, and it all would've looked straight-arrow."

"I was in a hurry."

"What else, kid? I can see something on your face and I've known you a long time. Spit it out."

"All right, here goes. The situation is that you've been hurt and now you're better. Which means that you're ready to go back to being the active President again."

"I know that, dammit, Tal! Put some more light between me and you."

"The situation has changed from when you told me to stop any likelihood of a secret attack against Cuba. It's changed for the better."

"How's that?"

"One point is that at some time when you were drugged against your will, Vice President Holt could've produced a paper and claimed you'd signed it at a time when you were actually out. That paper would've authorized a strike against Cuba and started World War Three going."

"I'm aware of that. It's one reason why I didn't snap your head off for taking me out of Walter Reed. Have you got any more fish on the fire?"

"Uh-huh. You've gained a lot of sympathy."

The President looked down at the site of his chest wound, but avoided remarking that the price for sympathy was almost too high. His brows were knotted in a frown.

"That's a change you could hang your hat on," he agreed finally. "Und so?"

"People will withhold judgment when you start acting up, start dropping some of the important ones mixed up in this caper, some who've been giving you advice but behind your back they've been cutting a deal for themselves."

"That's a game plan and a sound one," Garth Crosby decided. "But it'll get pretty auntsie-dancie around here for a while if I do it."

"That's what you want, though."

The vengeful streak in Garth Crosby that Renata had seen and painted was clear. This wasn't a matter of paying back somebody who'd shafted him in domestic politics, withheld a patronage plum or practiced discreet blackmail. All of those things Garth Crosby had done in his time, or he wouldn't have reached his current high office. This was a matter of blood, and the flare of his nostrils and curve of his lips showed just how well he knew it.

"This is not going to be easy," he said carefully, "but it has to be done. Tal, you're right. I'm in a better position now than at any other time since this trouble got started."

Tal knew that he had accepted the idea, and was waiting only to determine his priorities. He reached for the intercom.

"We'll do this my way, a little roundabout, Tal, and I'll need your help, as you'll see—I want to schedule a press conference for ten o'clock this morning." He smiled in satisfaction. "Pardon me, Tal, while I sharpen a long knife."

CHAPTER TWENTY-ONE

The intruder and chauffeur finally left the cheap apartment in which Renata was being held a prisoner. The man she knew as Venters came to the closed door of her room, opened it, looked in at her, pursed his lips, and then went off to another room and slammed the door on himself. She understood that he had wanted to take her by force, but couldn't do so because of the orders he had received from the second man; and he didn't want to take the chance of ruffling that particular one's feathers.

She saw no way of escaping. A chair had been tilted under the knob of her door and she knew she couldn't possibly disturb it in the dark without the chair falling. As for the front door, the chauffeur slept there on a cot.

"Damn it!"

First she thought that if she'd been left with a sketch pad and some soft pencils she wouldn't have considered anything else until she had gotten the scene down as firmly as possible. Then she told herself that she was being nothing less than a fool. What she needed to do was to use every resource in getting out.

But how?

Only the promise of dawn offered hope. She looked up at the coming sun, which would usually fascinate any artist, but not this time. She had seen dawns before, and would never try to paint one. That play of light could be useful in some portrait if she ever learned enough to imitate it.

Looking down to see the play of light on the sidewalk, an automatic gesture, she realized for the first time that she was only imprisoned on the floor above ground level.

Never in her life had she done anything like what she was planning. A jump this far down would be enough to kill an

older woman. She was aware of the possibility of hurting her
hands, as Venters himself had threatened to do.

But she wouldn't stay here now that she saw there might be
a choice; a difficult choice, a painful choice certainly, but she
would take it.

There was a sofa in the room, and one of the pillows was
half as large as her body. She would hold onto that pillow,
letting go at the last minute and keep the pillow under her
head and as much of the midriff as possible. She might injure
a leg that way, or even both legs; but the chance had to be
taken.

The window was locked, but only with the usual knob at
the top of the lower window interlocking with another knob.
She undid it instantly.

There was some chance that the window would squeak
when she tried to open it, alerting whomever was nearest—
the chauffeur, yes, she was too stirred up for clear thinking.
She would do it very easily.

The damn window did squeak. She inched it partway open
and waited to hear if there was any response. None. She
cursed the window in three languages, forgetting the profanity in English but recalling it vividly in French and German.
Again she eased it a little further up until there was the first
hint of a squeak and then she slowed the pace.

It took perhaps ten minutes. Dawn had been replaced by
morning light and people were coming out to the shabby
streets, probably leaving early for a day's work. There was
the hideous sound of a garbage truck; machinery crushing the
bags in its mechanical maw. A police siren could be heard,
then an ambulance. Over the sounds, annoying at any other
time, Renata accelerated the pace of opening the window.

It was done.

There could be no further reason for delay.

Just as she was fixing the pillow so that it would cover the
most vulnerable parts of herself, she heard footsteps in the
hallway. She couldn't delay for another second.

Renata climbed out to the ledge, straddling it with one foot
and then easing out the other so that it dangled in midair.

From some place a woman called out, "There's a crazy broad trying to jump."

"Oh, let her," somebody else responded. "Who the hell cares?"

Just as Renata heard the door to the room being pushed open in back of her she said a swift and silent prayer and released herself.

It was unbelievably quick. She let go of the pillow after less than two seconds in the cold air. The landing hurt, causing even her teeth to rattle. She had certainly scraped some of the meat off one leg and torn both stockings. She had wrenched a shoe. Her fingers though were unharmed, something she had been terribly anxious to avoid by this risky move. And she was alive.

"What the hell are you doing?" It was the chauffeur, shouting from above. She supposed he turned to notify Venters and both would be out here in seconds.

She tried to get up on her own power, but couldn't.

Above her a voice said helpfully, "Better stay until we can call an ambulance."

"A—a what?" She could hardly hear him because of the buzzing in her ears.

"A car to take you to the hospital." The man had spoken carefully, hearing the accented English.

"No, I must leave now."

"Are you sure? Looks to me like you could'a busted yourself good."

"I didn't." She raised a hand, lowered it to the hard sidewalk—only then did she realize that the invaluable foam rubber pillow had rolled away after the impact. The man reluctantly helped her stand.

She was dizzy, putting both hands before her face as if to anchor herself.

"I must hire a cab."

The man, who was middle-aged, looked doubtful. "Hard to say if I should let you go, Miss. Maybe you don't understand what I been saying."

Luckily, some other people had been attracted by the

aftermath of her jump, many of them young men. Venters
and his helper would think twice about starting more trouble.

"You're not an American," one of the men said. And,
hopefully, "*Parlez-vous Francais?* I did some time in the
Army over there and haven't used the lingo since then."

The last thing Renata wanted to do was to play games. She
gathered her forces as best she could. "I have to get a cab.
Can you phone for one? It is urgent."

The middle-aged man spoke. "Better call for an ambulance instead. This young lady might be in trouble."

"I tell you I'm not!"

"Well, I won't have it on my conscience that I let a girl go
away after she jumped out a second floor window."

"I don't know that she's wrong," one of the women put
in. "You take a baby, now. My sister Maud's little one, three
years old, he fell out a window of their place near Lake
Michigan in Evanston, Illinois."

The location was plainly a source of pride. "Picked himself up and laughed. Sound as a nut, that boy. Didn't even do
in his diapers."

Renata wondered if she wasn't losing her mind. "I feel
perfectly well, perfectly well."

She was looking around for a taxi and spotted one that
turned off into another street. But it gave hope that another
might come. She looked in that direction only, a hand ready
to be raised.

The man continued, "This girl can't be well! She just
jumped out of a window! All I want—"

"I know what you want," a young girl called out. "And so
does every woman in three miles of here! Old enough to be
her father, and you ought to be ashamed of yourself."

There was a cruising cab on the corner. Renata couldn't
start for it because the older man was firmly gripping her by
the other hand to keep her from falling. She raised a hand,
waving it frantically. The cabbie started down the street.
Renata didn't know if he was coming toward her, but she
allowed herself to feel hopeful. This wasn't a main street or a

large one and any cruising cab driver would go in a different direction.

The cab stopped at the northwest corner. A door opened, and a man and a woman got out. The woman looked sympathetically over at Renata while the man was paying. Renata kept waving like a fool, hoping she had caught the driver's eye and attention.

Behind her, the discussion kept on. "Men are all alike, always ready to take advantage of a girl if she's in even the least trouble."

"The least! Why, this girl—"

"Male chauvinist pig!"

A man said philosphically, "The answer to that is 'female chauvinist sow,' but it doesn't add any light to the argument."

"Let 'er go! Get your lunch hooks off her!"

"Yes, let her go so she'll fall over and show these dumb broads what's what."

Renata, who had been quietly blessing the cause of women's lib, knew that she probably would lose her balance without support. But once more, luck was with her. The driver was opening his rear door from the inside and she reached out gratefully for it. Her rescuer let her go.

She smiled graciously at him and said, "Thank you very much," causing the women to look disappointed while the men showed pleasure.

A woman's voice said angrily, "It's the girls themselves who let down other women! That's how it goes, always!"

The cab drove away, the driver asking her destination.

"The White House," she said weakly. "Immediately."

She'd arrange for him to be paid as she didn't have any money on her, and would shortly be in touch with Tal. She knew he had taken Garth Crosby there, and that as a result he must be available to her.

She didn't settle back for the drive.

CHAPTER TWENTY-TWO

The press conference was held in the East Room, the President standing at a polished lectern on the podium. Television lights glared at him. The questions came thick and fast; the President accepting them because the statement he had wanted to read wasn't written down yet.

The questions about his health were quickly asked and easily handled. Tal, watching, saw his half brother deal tactfully with a question about pornography.

"I don't approve of laws which empower citizens to make arrests of pornographers because individuals aren't judges of the morals of others. As for community initiatives, it strikes me that a book might be published and sell well in Cleveland and get the writer jailed in Laramie." He looked irritably in Tal's direction, left of the stage, but no statement was forthcoming about Cuba.

Tal was called to the phone, answering only because he hoped it involved that damned statement about Cuba. It didn't. Hubert Horton, the evangelist who had been so helpful a few days ago, was on the line. He wanted to speak with the President, wishing him well. Tal assumed that he was in earshot of wealthy patrons, wanting to prove to them that he was the confidant of those in power. Tal spoke briskly, but did Horton the favor of saying he would notify the President of the call.

His next message was from Renata Waye, who was at the White House gate. Tal, not able to leave at this particular time, was relieved to hear she hadn't been harmed. He explained that he couldn't come out himself, but would send somebody else and would see her as soon as the press conference was over.

By that time Garth Crosby was answering questions about

establishing a space colony of some ten thousand people to orbit the earth at the same distance from it as from the moon.

"The annual cost of the project would be about three times that of Project Apollo—the manned lunar landings," he said. "It is planned to get about ninety percent of construction material from the moon and supply it to the colony by a system of space propulsion. The station would be over three thousand feet long, with its axis aimed toward the sun. Mirrored panels on the sides would swing open and reflect sunlight into the cylinder for twelve hours a day. A parabolic reflector at the end of the cylinder would focus sunlight onto a power generator."

"What about food?" Another reporter asked. "How much would be sufficient to feed each person in a space colony, Mr. President?"

"I'm a little hazy on that, myself," Garth Crosby began modestly and then answered in detail about drains thriving in sunlight and the intentions to grow some plants in Styrofoam and feed goats some vegetable matter as a source of milk. He was in the middle of the discourse when Tal received a signal from the press secretary and a sheet was pressed into his hand. It was the statement on Cuba, as corrected for typographical errors. Tal read it swiftly, nodded, then gave it to the President.

Garth managed to read the vital statement while speaking about the chances of aiming laser beams at rocket engines in flight from mountain tops to heat them. He interrupted himself immediately.

"If I might bring us down to earth for just a few minutes, ladies and gentlemen," the President said carefully. "I would like to discuss the relations of the United States with its neighbor, Cuba.

"This country is not happy that Cuba has had a communist government chosen for it. We are certainly not happy that the Russians are giving aid, both covert and overt, to that government. Nor are we pleased that the Cuban government as seen fit to send soldiers into war in other countries with hopes to convert those countries to what it calls Communism. And we are upset that the Castro government as been flooding this country with more immigrants than we can handle from any one source. I want to be clear about this, clear and unmistakable in my meaning.

"The United States has no intention of going to war with the Cuban government over these matters. We will bend every effort to be good neighbors, and to settle our differences with the Cuban government in a peaceful fashion."

In the flurry of questions that followed, Tal heard a commotion to his right. He looked out and saw Renata in the hall. Convinced that if the press secretary couldn't help Garth in a pinch he himself could do nothing at all, he hurried out.

"Honey," he whispered and surprised himself by embracing her in public.

She was breathing raggedly, but able to talk clearly. "I wasn't harmed," she repeated, happy at his concern for her. "I am well."

"Let's go to the cabinet room and have a drink sent in for you," he said after a moment. "We have a lot of talking to do."

He settled her in one of the soft chairs. There was a scratch on her left cheek and her stockings were torn. She decided that it was too early for a drink and that she didn't want to see Dr. Mellors; but she accepted black coffee and Tal joined her in the combination of coffee-and-chicory that both he and the President favored.

"You were kidnapped and held overnight," Tal said, summarizing what she'd told him. "One man was named Venters and you say he claimed to be a salesman of defense items but that Venters wasn't his real name. A mean looking guy with a black beard and in his forties. And he has a wife and two children."

"Yes."

"I don't know him myself, but I'm sure he can be rooted out." Tal made a mental note to speak with Alva Congalton. "There was another man who drove the kidnap car, but who you don't know otherwise and didn't see too closely."

"Yes." She shuddered mildly.

"I suppose your friend works with somebody or there's someone so close to him that he's not afraid of trusting him. A bunch of bastards!"

"Yes. When I think of what could've happened, I feel sick."

"Now the third one, Renata. Let's give him a little thought. You say he has a red face and is probably in his thirties. Did you notice anything else about him?"

"He has sandy hair."

"Ah." It was no time to tell her how glad he was that she observed people's features. "Did you see enough of him to notice his eyes?"

"Hardly. I was behind a door, as I have said, and I only had a second to see him, but he blinked oddly."

"Few of us can judge time correctly, Renata, so I'd suppose you had more than a second. Concentrate on the eyes, Renata. Did you form any impression of them?"

"None that I retain."

"Let's see if I can't help." Tal ran a hand through his blond hair. "Was this bastard in the sun when you saw him?"

"No."

"So his eyes weren't blinking from the sudden sunlight?"

"Quite the contrary. It was nighttime."

He hid his anger, and supposed that in her confusion she hadn't been clear herself, let alone making the image unmistakable to him. "The room wasn't well lit then? So he had no reason to blink away light when he walked in."

"None at all. But—yes—his eyes were half-shut for longer than a second."

"Our friend might have drooping eyelids, then. That is, they droop all the time."

"Perfectly possible, now that you cause me to remember it." Renata was surprised. "Do you know who he is, Tal? I am sure he was very much a man of influence."

"Yes, I think that's true. Does the name Eugene Vale mean anything to you."

"Most certainly not." She bridled. "I know little about American life."

"True enough," he said, affable now that part of the problem was solved. "Drink your slumgullion and eat your hardtack—" he was referring to the buttered toast she had requested "—while I do a little high-class thinking."

He was remembering Eugene Vale. Gene had become an Intelligence success story, in most people's opinion.

He had entered the Intelligence services fresh out of college and worked in the Tasking Office, followed by stints in photo, signals, and what was called Human Intelligence. He had gone from Collection Evaluation to Current Operations, where he was considered a dependable man with a highly developed sense of protective coloration. An operator who could cover his ass on any and all occasions.

Certainly he was considered a middle-of-the-road man. He had no reputation for having been an extremist, for being a wild-eyed dreamer who was certain that Communists were under every bush and tree. But he didn't minimize the Communist influence or importance, either. He had a genuine loathing for them and it was coupled with a full appreciation of the damage they had already done in the world and the damage they could still do. A combatant during the Vietnam War, he fully detested the Viet Communists and understood how badly they had affected their area of the world. Nor was he a wide-eyed innocent in dealing with the Chinese.

As for the Cubans, Vale was tight-lipped in his dislike of them. Once he had explained that his mother had lived in Key West before the gays turned it into an outpost of Fire Island in New York. Tal hadn't bothered to correct any of those dogmatic remarks, but couldn't deny that Key West was only ninety damn miles from Fidel.

So the problem was clear. The Vice President of the United States and Gene Vale were with others in the military establishment and Intelligence who wanted an all-out war against Cuba. They had arranged for the President to be shot in hopes of taking advantage to start the action that they craved.

And they had to be dealt with. Quickly. . .

Tal stood up and left the room. He walked into the President's study. Garth Crosby was stretched out on a cot. He

was obeying Dr. Mellors' instructions and being irritable
while he was at it. Having concluded the press conference, he
took the doctor's advice about resting even though he felt
well.

"My body doesn't need a rest," he grumbled. "You
know, I think my wife is right about doctors; they think the
human body is a machine and don't take account of feeling
good or bad. Ten years ago when I was forty-some, I told Vic
Mellors that I felt I was losing control of my life and was very
jittery for that reason. Know what he said? 'Don't think about
it,' that's what he said. That's his idea of medical advice
without pills. When I leave this job, Loretta's going to find a
doctor with a holistic approach and then—well, Tal, what's
up? You're not interested in my feeling good while I have to
make believe I'm an invalid. What *are* you interested in,
then?"

"You're going to hate my guts," Tal said when he had
closed the door on the President and himself. "It's about
those bastards wanting an invasion of Cuba."

"What about it? Are you trying to tell me you're on *their*
side now?"

"Garth, I think there has to be an invasion of Cuba for
purely domestic reasons, and there's no time to lose," Tal
said.

Garth Crosby sat up straight on his cot, ignoring the flick
of mild pain across his midsection.

"Well, I'll be damned," the President said when his half
brother had concluded. "I'll be well and truly damned."

"You understand why you've got to go through with it?"
Tal pressed him.

Instead of answering directly, the President said, "You'd
have been a big success in politics, Tal. You're a bigger louse
than I am."

Tal understood. The plan had been approved. Reluctantly,
but it had been approved.

CHAPTER TWENTY-THREE

"Of course it was camouflage," the President said tiredly. "I've had this in mind all the time."

"I wish we had known," said Admiral Janes, letting out a deep relieved breath. "It would've saved us all a lot of heartburn and suspicions about your Americanism, Mr. President, if I might say so."

An hour had passed. Tal had sent Renata to the Hay Adams on Sixteenth Street, having asked a Secret Service man who owed him a favor to escort her. The President had called a meeting of those he had good reason to believe were unscrupulously in favor of an all-out war with Cuba.

"Thank you, Fred," the President said to Janes, nodding his head. "I hope I've cleared up matters with you others, as well."

"It's unfortunate," said Eugene Vale, running five fingers over his Indian-red face, "that we didn't have any indication of this."

Janes answered for the President. "We're all in Washington, where everybody gossips. If the President had let out word one on Tuesday, all of Washington would know it by Wednesday."

"Exactly," the President said. "And that thought leads to my next point."

"We're certainly listening most attentively," Janes said, his body at attention even though he was seated.

Garth Crosby smiled. Janes had continued his military career in spite of a medical record with hair-raising aspects. Striken by ileitis, ("Eisenhower's illness," as he often said proudly), he wasn't helped sufficiently by cortisone and had to be operated on, his doctors taking out several feet of intestine and stapling him up, as the process was called. He had survived the operation, and even managed to make sour little jokes about being in the intensive care unit with terminal cases and a deranged patient who had twice thrown a filled bedpan at him. Janes had taken a three-month leave to recover and was back at his job. It was rare, though, in these first weeks back that anybody could keep him from talking about his recent illness. Apparently it took the promise of war to keep him from that.

Everett Maloney of CIA Polly Ann section, as political analysis was called because the letters alone as an identification would have been confusing, was in the room as well. By rank he was Vale's superior; a swarthy man with ice-cold eyes, who looked around repeatedly as if to be sure who he could blame if this material was leaked.

"My next point is that I want the invasion staged as quickly as possible," President Crosby said. "I want a date decided on before this conference is over."

General Davis nodded. "My troops can be ready in a week." He was a tall, bronzed man with the smallest mouth a grown human could have, or so his friends said.

The admiral said, "Likewise."

"Good," Davis nodded. "And we'll have as many back-up people ready as will be required."

"I want everybody who participates in this to be a volunteer, somebody who wants this invasion to succeed with all his heart and soul and would do everything to make sure it does."

"Volunteers only," Vale murmured. "That will cut down heavily on staff."

"Nevertheless it is a condition I insist upon."

"It'll be done, of course," the admiral promised.

Davis nodded.

The door opened on Edward Holt, the Vice President striding into the room ten minutes late, which was usual with him. Astonished by what he'd heard, his mouth open, Holt paused before sitting down. He looked fit as ever, and except for one venomous glance at Tal, who was sitting quietly beyond the cabinet table, he seemed otherwise unruffled.

Holt, having understood what was being said, responded to the President's questioning look. "I won't bother you with any oratorical crap, Mr. President, but I'm very happy to know that you've understood what we were all blatting about."

"Oh, I've understood that much from the start."

"It surprises me that you didn't take advantage of being out of commission for a few days to let me arrange what was necessary and put it through."

"I felt that the buck should stop here, as old Harry Truman always said." Garth considered. "It's been decided that the action will begin, Ed, in seven days, and that there'll be a sufficient backup to make sure it doesn't fail."

"Something else," the general said quietly. "I didn't plan to bring this up, but I think it is a matter of—I don't put this too strongly, sir—a matter of national honor. I was in the service when President Kennedy put his backing behind the Bay of Pigs effort although, as you are aware, he withdrew air support from the carrier *Essex*, as I think it was, at the last."

"Yes, general."

"As a result, America became something of a laughing stock to the world. Unjustly, I may add. Having helped to draw up plans for the effort, though only in a preliminary fashion, I feel that I—that we all in this country—have to regain our prestige."

Garth Crosby didn't dare let himself look past the table to where his half brother was sitting. "If I understand it correctly, general, you are proposing to repeat the Bay of Pigs strategy at this time."

"I am, sir. With, of course, up-to-date modifications such as lasers, STEALTH planes, and whatever else may be necessary."

Garth Crosby said, "I believe that during World War Two, Winston Churchill felt that Germany's ill-gotten territories should have been re-taken in the order in which they had originally been stolen, so there's some historical precedent for what you're suggesting."

"Modern equipment, eh?" Edward Holt's eyes lit up. The sportsman Vice President said, "I'd like to be out there with you boys."

"You're welcome aboard, Mr. Vice President, far as I'm concerned," responded the general.

"No, we'll have none of that," Garth said to the Vice President. "You have to realize, Ed, that you're too valuable to risk."

Edward Holt subsided, but didn't like the idea of accepting the decision. He had often been insubordinate, and now he was imagining himself at the head of the successful warriors of this new invasion, and as a result, being a sure bet for the Presidency when Garth Crosby's last term ran out. He glared around the table, then glowered at Tal Lion sitting quietly.

"Very well, Mr. President. It's your ball game," the Vice President said.

But everyone in the room knew well that Edward Holt would do his best to short-circuit the President's order and make the trip, somehow. No one knew how, but with the force of Holt's personality it seemed more than likely.

Holt said with care, "I take it that your mind has been made up on this matter for a long time, Mr. President, and so has Mr. Lion's."

"What has Tal got to do with policy?" the President asked.

"Well, let me get at it another way." He had been a successful lawyer in his home state. Now he paused to phrase the point differently. "Mr. Lion supports your policies."

"He implements them," the President said carefully, not hiding his irritation well enough. "Really, Ed, I haven't got the slightest idea what Tal's opinions have to do with this."

"Why, it's simply this, Mr. President. If you support the venture, Mr. Lion should be prepared to help."

"Certainly."

"And since the troops are to be made up of volunteers who passionately believe in the cause, I take it that he, too, will be one of those volunteers."

Holt looked over carefully at Tal, most likely expecting to

see him turn pale. Tal, however, was smiling widely.

Garth said smoothly, "If I can spare him for the duty, Ed, you can be pretty sure that Talbot Lion will make the scene."

"Mr. President," Holt said quietly, "that's not quite good enough, if I might be pardoned for making the point. We have a saying in Montana—"

The President bridled.

Tal Lion put in pleasantly, "I feel sure I'll be there, Mr. Vice President. If it's at all possible, in fact, I plan to make a distinct point of being there."

The gauntlet had been dropped, and each man understood the other. Holt would be at the scene of battle and avenge himself for Tal's beating him in the combat at his Watergate apartment. Tal would, on his side, be alert and ready for the private battle.

"Yes, indeed, Mr. Lion," Holt purred. "You're a man after my own heart."

"That," Tal Lion responded with just as much insincerity, "is deeply gratifying to me."

Garth Crosby, having caught the by-play, said quietly, "I think, then, gentlemen, that we can consider the meeting concluded."

Almost with one motion, the other participants got up and moved quietly to the door.

CHAPTER TWENTY-FOUR

"I have no intention of letting you go out there," the President said. "You have to stay in the continental United States and get into the only business that's right for you, when my term is up."

"And what business is that?" Tal asked.

"The only line of work for you is as a whoremaster," the President said lightly, purposely using the old-fashioned word.

Tal came back at him with a current expression. "That would mellow me out, for sure."

Loretta Crosby spoke irritably about the lack of decorum in the White House. They were in the residential dining room, its ceiling redesigned in up-ended squares like a harlequin's costume. When Loretta left to pick up her knitting in the Lincoln Room, the President spoke more pointedly.

"You've got no insurance, Tal, that Ed Holt won't search you out and kill you under the cover of battle, and you know it."

"True enough, but Holt hasn't got any insurance against my killing him if he tries that." Tal shrugged. "He has to be stopped, and Cochinos Bay is going to be a good place to do it."

"Yes." The President shuddered. "You know I've got a ruthless streak in me that orders this sort of operation with the greatest pleasure."

"I've noticed." Tal tried to put his half brother at ease by joking about something he didn't really think was funny. "I'm a bastard, that's true, but you're a *bastard!*"

"Needs must when the devil drives," Renata murmured. "That is one of your American sayings, yes?"

Tal stirred in bed next to her. "One of them."

"In that case, I shall marry," Renata said with more firmness than she had suspected was in her. "I am becoming too fond of you. I know I will soon feel that I want to paint your portrait and when that happens with a lover I am losing control of myself."

"Marry who?" He listed possibilities in easy mockery. "A butcher or baker or candlestick maker will be damned dull after these few months with me."

"Excitement isn't everything."

He flicked away that point. "It *is* till you're forty, at a guess. Both of us have a good way to go."

Her response was prompt and unmistakable. "I need a settled man with a good business."

"I know a widower who's only got twelve children, and he's awfully damned tired." He grinned. "And I'm not sure he can do things like—well, *this*, for instance!"

"Oh, Tal!"

"And I doubt if he ever did this—or this—and I almost forgot *this*."

"Tal, that's good!"

"Now what do you think of me?"

"Tal, Tal, you son-of-a-bitch," she said happily.

Later, in a drowse she murmured, "I forgot to tell you that I checked out the Dulles Airport and your plane is back from Turkey. It was flown in a day ago."

"And just in time," he said, sitting up slowly. "Saved me a job, that check of yours."

"Do you mean that we're going off again?"

"Not the two of us this time. Just me."

Concern darkened Renata's eyes. "Another mission?"

"Yes, and a hell of a complicated one."

"Is there any chance that I might not see you again?" she whispered.

"There sure is a chance, baby."

"Must you go?"

He considered soberly. There was no point to saying that Edward Holt's career, if unchecked, might be harmful to the country. He was willing to murder at war and in private, both. He was one of those rare amoral types who occasionally crept into politics, and could usually be squelched by others of his kind. But not always. In the precarious balance of current politics, a figure like Holt could take on another Children's Crusade and destroy three-quarters of the known world. He had to be stopped. Garth Crosby had felt sure he'd keep the man under his thumb in the vice presidency, but it hadn't worked. There was only one answer left now, a pretty damnable answer.

"Yes, Renata, I must go."

She said quietly, "I will not begin a portrait of you now, or make sketches. But when you come back—if you do—then, my dear, Tal, perhaps."

He understood. Renata wasn't the type, any more than Tal himself was, to say *I love you*, in so many words. He had too much respect for Renata to touch her idly now, and after a few innocuous words he left.

A girl mechanic named Sheila Downey, who had serviced his plane over the last few years when he was at Dulles, stood talking to him about the *Explorer*. With its orange wings glittering in the October sun and in back of them, the plane reminded Tal of a medical patient hearing a relative get the news.

There was some possible trouble with the shock absorber system in the main landing gear, so that the control might not be as effective as it ought to be. Tal contributed an observation of the drooping tail, which in itself could produce a slight shimmy in midair. There wasn't much time to do the work they both felt was needed, at least not all of it. Sheila Downey promised to do the job. She was a tall woman with good muscles and light hair. A few years ago she had been good looking. Somebody told Tal once that she'd been repeatedly raped in her childhood by a neighborhood policeman, and Tal hoped she'd stamped the man to death when she had her full growth and strength. She looked as if she might have done it.

"Long flight, Mr. Lion?"

"Another one, yes."

"Well, you're certain to make stopovers on the way, then. You've programmed for that in the past and you'll do it this time, too. If she gets cranky, the mechanics at the other fields can give her the colic medicine."

"Good thinking, in case something isn't done a hundred percent on this trip, which heaven forbid." He smiled. "There's at least one more reason for making occasional stopovers." She looked surprised and questioning. He said, "No bathroom on the *Explorer*."

"True enough." She turned away.

"Well, if I have to, I can open the door part way and aim out."

She glanced back. For the first time he had the satisfaction of seeing the liberated Sheila Downey blushing to the ears.

Gene Vale's office was large and well-planned. A framed photograph of a small girl showed on the desk. Vale, settling himself, caught Tal's eye on the child's brightly complected face.

"She hardly knows me any more," he complained softly. "Thinks the sun rises and sets on her mother."

Tal observed that there was no other family photograph on the desk. "Separated?"

"For eight months now, her mother and I have been separated. Of course she took Melanie with her. The job was the major culprit, with its off-hours. And then just as a sign of her intellectual independence, my wife turned against everything that the agency stands for. And I mean everything. Whatever your opinion of the CIA might be, and I would think that any intelligent outsider's is mixed, her stance is as wrongheaded as being in favor of the agency's operations blindly."

"Agreed," Tal said sincerely, and changed the subject. He didn't want to know anything about Gene Vale's private life. "About the operation we're all involved with. Let's give that some of our time right now."

"Yes." Vale settled further into his chair. "Decisions

have been made of which I don't entirely approve, but politics change colorations."

"What are you saying, Vale? In English, now."

"It, the operation, is to seem like a Cuban one, a revolt. Just like the original Bay of Pigs back in April of '61."

"That means there'll be Cuban volunteers on the line for us."

"Yes. They're hopping anxious to go, I can tell you that much. They've been planning to get rid of Fidel since he took over, and I'm sorry to say that in some cases their fathers planned, too." He considered. "There's a type of person, man or woman, who is political and has to leave his country for that reason, then spends the rest of life pretending to still be a force in that country's future. Sometimes they're right."

"As in this case," Tal said sententiously. "What about the weaponry?"

"Most of it is to be along the same lines as that used back in '61."

"Most but not all?"

"I'm pretty sure that at least one man involved with the sale of current weaponry to the Armed Forces will be on a ship." Vale smiled. "A particularly good friend of mine, who I think has met Renata Waye also."

Tal made a point of chuckling. He knew that the man who'd called himself Venters was being mentioned.

"You must introduce me to that guy sometime," he said mildly enough. "I'd like to meet him."

"Mr. Lion, I am ashamed of my defective hospitality," said Ignor Gurianov. The black-bearded master spy regretted not having been able to invite Tal to his home. "My apartment is in a good section and comfortably furnished as well, so I enjoy permitting my few capitalist friends to make their little jokes."

The two were in the open air, on H Street. To one side as they walked was the Naval Museum, Decatur House loomed on the other.

"But I have no choice," Gurianov continued. "You tell

me that you wish to speak of important matters and some device to make a record of conversations could have been implanted there."

"By our side or yours," Tal said agreeably in spite of the tension that rode him. "Or you might be carrying something along that line in one of your pockets."

"Or *you* might," Gurianov pointed out. "Have we now exhausted the major possibilities and may we discuss whatever business you feel that we have?"

"Certainly." Tal lowered his voice. "Gurianov, there is a matter in which the two of us should be allies."

"And that matter is?"

"It involves preventing an all-out war."

The Russian considered, then put a hand into one pocket long enough to disconnect a recording machine. "I hope that later on we will record something innocuous, you and I, in case I should be observed in your company and have to explain the nature of the discussion. My people are possessed of enormous curiosity."

"I understand." Tal waited.

Gurianov resumed the thread of conversation, but not until he had looked hastily around the street. "There are militants on our side as well as yours. Those on your side could soon gain the upper hand."

Tal didn't see the struggle for world domination that the Communists were waging as any contest with two equal sides; but he passed the point over for the moment.

"Mr. Lion, what are you proposing to do about it and why at this time?"

Tal gave him that information.

"So you feel that I and my government can help by making the necessary contacts." Gurianov saw the bad temper reflected on Tal's features. "Mr. Lion, I do not fence with words at this difficult time. You realize, however that I can, on my own, agree to nothing. All I can do is get in touch with my government, and convey your request."

"Suppose you have to do more?" Tal asked. "Let's assume your government tells you to do nothing because the

militants in your country have taken greater control? What
then? You'll let it all go and take chances on World War
Three?''

"Mr. Lion, I could not take a short cut on the necessary
communications.''

"You could if it's necessary," Tal said with finality.
"What I want to know is whether you will do it—again, if
that's necessary.''

They walked half a block in silence. Gurianov broke it.

"Mr. Lion, I wish capitalism no good because my government does not, and I actively work against the capitalist
system because I am a Soviet citizen and see it as my duty.
But I lost many relatives in Hitler's war, though I was very
young indeed at the time, and will not permit such a disaster
to befall my country again if I can in any way stop it. That is
your answer.''

"So we're allies after all," Tal Lion said. "Reluctantly,
but allies.''

"Yes, Mr. Lion, we are indeed allies.''

CHAPTER TWENTY-FIVE

Vice President Edward Holt said quietly, "Talbot Lion isn't here."

Admiral Janes agreed, "Not on this ship, certainly."

The *Merriweather,* one of six ships, was steaming ahead for the Bay of Pigs and due to arrive at dawn. Edward Holt, on the ship despite President Crosby's orders to avoid the expedition, paced the deck furiously.

"He damn well promised, and I took his word."

Janes snapped, "That's your hang-up, Mr. Holt. You're anxious to settle a score, if Washington gossip is correct. I'm anxious to get my ships to Cochinos."

"If Lion is on any of the other boats, let me know."

"I will."

Eugene Vale, on board the *Sealion* was speaking to the man Renàta Waye knew as Venters.

"You came because there's some advanced weaponry with us and you know it," he said thinly.

Venters had expected to be sick as a dog but wasn't. Instead he felt regrets at leaving his family.

"Think of this as just another road trip," Vale snapped. "We're a hundred percent safe up here. Nothing will go wrong."

Vale had good reason to be satisfied. Plans had moved forward easily and smoothly. Cuban exiles and refugees, all of them militant, had been training for such an expedition over the last few years. The plan was for them to go ashore under an umbrella of U.S. air support, and get to the Sierra Escambray, which was some one hundred miles from the place where they'd be landing. With control of that much territory, the Cubans could then declare that they had formed a provisional government and ask for and obtain help from the United States. Nothing could be simpler. It was the Bay of Pigs all over again, but successful this time, as the original invasion would have been if John Kennedy hadn't seen fit at the last moment to withdraw air support. Well, somebody had to go in and pull the politicians' chestnuts out of the fire.

Before they reached the landing area, U.S. planes with Cuban markings would've bombed airfields at Santiago, at Baracoa, and at San Antonio de los Banos, smashing most of Castro's air force and MIGs that the Russians had sent him.

"Everything will be okay," Vale said, and stopped to read a telex just handed to him. He shrugged and tore it up, then shook his head.

"Holt is having all sorts of blue fits because Talbot Lion didn't make it at the last minute," he said, then frowned. "I wonder what the hell did happen to Lion."

Venters, looking for another possible source of jitters, said, "Do you suppose Lion has some information to prove we're going to miss out?"

"Lion couldn't know a single solitary bit more than I do," Vale boasted. "That much is for sure."

Rosendo Salguero, the Cuban leader whose name was considered first in enlisting support for this effort, smiled engagingly. He was a large, soft-spoken man whose father had fought Batista and hailed Castro during the first weeks. As soon as the direction of Fidel's government had become unmistakably clear, the elder Salguero declared his opposition, took his family to Puerto Rico, and then to the American mainland. The younger Salguero had promised the father on the latter's deathbed that the fight against the *barbudos* would be continued, and had risen to a place of eminence among the Cuban exiles in the Americas. Like his father before him, the younger Salguero was sure of himself, arrogant, and a good man to have at your side in a fight against odds.

"This has been settled at the correct time," he said. "The last minute, in effect."

"How do you mean?" General Davis asked. They were on board the *Magnificent*, the newest of the ships to be given this assignment.

"The United States is doing its duty," Salguero said, "just before the Cuban patriots resolved to commit terrorist actions."

"In Cuba, you mean?"

"No, general, in the United States." Salguero smiled. "We had come to feel that only by terror on the mainland could the United States be moved to do what is painfully necessary to help our own poor homeland. The fist! Hit hard and often so that the United States will send and support troops sent into Cuba, and declare the necessary preventative war."

Davis looked angry.

Salguero smiled. "But now your wise President, sensing the Cuban mood and that of many Americans, has shown that such action is unnecessary. He has declared himself a true partner and is giving us the chance to fight with vigor for our homeland."

Davis turned away as an aide came in with a telex. He responded briefly, but was distracted upon looking back.

"Where in the hell's hinges is he?" the general murmured.

"Pardon?"

"Talbot Lion promised to be on this expedition and isn't here," the general said, chewing part of his upper lip briefly. "I don't like that."

"Mr. Lion?" Salguero searched his excellent memory. "The blond young man, you mean. An aide of your President's. Yes. He is not to do the fighting, so it matters little. We Cubans are to do that, with air support from the United States."

"Exactly, but—"

"He is not required."

"True enough."

"Then there is no need to be in distress."

"I wouldn't say that. Lion isn't a fellow who breaks his

promises. He takes a certain pride in following through to the letter if he accepts an obligation. I really don't like his absence.''

''But you cannot tell me the exact reason for your feeling?''

''Correct.''

''Then all you can do, general, is to make sure that everything necessary is done.''

''I have already. More than once.''

That exchange was enough to convince Davis that Salguero had the necessary qualities of a leader. It wasn't enough to be a strong tactician and know one's native land well. The ability to see what was essential made for the key to leadership.

Salguero stood. ''I go to join those of my troops who are on this ship with me. We are all returning to the homeland, that land we dearly love and in which many of our relatives have been tortured and burned and killed. Returning is an experience that unnerves a man, you see. I want to comfort the troops, and they will then perform with greater skill.''

''Yes, Mr. Salguero, I understand that.''

The Cuban left. Davis found himself feeling angry all over again at the Cuban's threats of terrorism on the United States mainland. Then he considered if the military reputation of his country could be regained by a few quick but fully supported operations in Vietnam. He would put the case for such an effort to President Crosby, a man who seemed sympathetic to military considerations. That made for one blessed change in a United States' President.

Remembering the President caused General Davis to wonder once more what under the sun had happened to Talbot Lion. Again he decided, without knowing just why, that he felt very slightly uneasy.

The ships made their rendezvous three miles south of Cienfuegos. At that point the landing craft was dispatched to the mainland. Six so-called battalions of men, each numbering two hundred, were on the LCT's. From his vantage point two thousand yards offshore a little before dawn, Admiral Janes saw the craft bobbing and weaving through the coral.

At his signal the ships began pounding the darkness with seventy-five millimeter shells. At the same time, other LCT's with supplies and ammunition reserves were on the way to go with the others.

Watching on board *Merriweather*, Edward Holt said, "They'd better pull it off this time. We won't give 'em another chance."

"Let's hope they do it," Janes said.

"What are my chances for getting on shore in one of the ships and seeing a little of the action?" Holt asked.

"Your chances, Mr. Vice President? Non-existent."

"Now look here—"

"On ship, Mr. Holt, I am in command. From that vantage I tell you that you won't be permitted to do so."

"No ifs, ands, or buts?"

"Not unless something completely unforeseen were to happen."

And in moments, the counterattack was under way.

Over the roar of cannon fire, Venters tried to make himself understood. The *Sealion* was pitching very slightly, and it didn't help.

"How will we know if the new stuff works?"

"When the Army goes down three roads to the Escambray," Vale shouted back. "This is the big go-round, all right!"

Venters said, "I ought to be on shore."

"We can't take the chance of a Yank being grabbed by Castro."

"I'll stay with the troops."

"Mistakes happen, and prisoners get taken even from winning armies."

Venters suddenly winced. "God, what's that?" The ship had pitched so hard he'd nearly lost his footing, and this occurred at a time when the guns were silent.

"Look upstairs," Gene Vale said grimly. "We're in for a fight."

On board the *Magnificent*, General Davis squinted up at the sky. He saw Soviet MIG planes, the biggest and best of the hardware that the Russians had given Castro. The planes—impossible to see how many of them there were— dived and strafed; the bullets shaving the ship so that she was becoming almost a collection of metal slivers.

Davis' adjutant rushed to him. "General, we have to get away from the deck *muy pronto*."

"Not just yet." No one had ever said that Davis wasn't a brave man.

"General, you have to get away, I tell you! It's absolutely necessary."

Davis watched a bomb fall harmlessly into the water and knew that not every one of them would do no damage.

"Are there lifeboats? See that the sailors bail out, if the captain isn't available. And put Maloney on a boat, too." Everett Maloney, the other CIA man to come out with Gene Vale, had insisted on taking the same ship as his friend, Davis. In a quieter voice he said, "If Lion was here, I'd drown him."

"Sir?"

"Castro got on to this so quickly that somebody had to tip him off. It was Talbot Lion who did that."

Vale had reached the same conclusion. "This damn Lion did it," he said as he and Venters joined others in a run for the lifeboats. The *Sealion* shook like a leaf under the impact of one bomb, and canted even as Vale lost his footing. Venters was nursing a bruised leg.

The ship, with the others, had tried to withdraw. It couldn't move. Planes and bombs made it impossible to go anywhere. The only recourse was to man the lifeboats and then to head for Cuba's shores.

Sailors crowding into the lifeboats, all of them volunteers who had been eager to move ahead on the mission, cursed as they waited for room. They had been well-trained and knew the advantages of orderly retreat. Venters, who didn't curse often, heard the sort of profanity that was known only to youngsters.

"How'd I get into this?"

"Shut up and—oh, Christ!"

A plane had passed overhead. Venters saw it briefly. Vale, hoping to get information about the shape, though he didn't know what he'd do with it, had a longer look. Both saw the bomb in the air. Venters was already scuttling off as the bomb whistled and impacted. He saw a galaxy of colors and then felt something painful smash his back.

He was gasping in pain when one of the enemy planes flew overhead, made a brief pass and put him out of his misery with two bullets. One struck in the arm and flew to his heart ventricle, killing him instantly. The other, crashed into his temple, just above the left ear.

Gene Vale made his way into one of the lifeboats just as the fire started. He ought to have gone to his stateroom for a jacket, but that was risky at such a time. It was one risk or the other, and he had chosen to be mobile and get into one of the last boats. The *Sealion*—was already listing and he didn't have the least notion how much longer it could stay up. He was huddled with the other survivors when one of the fighters made one more sweep overhead.

Swiftly estimating the chances, Vale felt it could go one way or the other. There was some chance of surviving this brush-by but not every one that would follow. With dawn coming, the odds in the fighters' and bombers' favor grew bigger. Vale decided he was as good as dead. A life jacket might have given him more of a chance, but not much. One of those bullets had his name on it.

He had made the wrong choice, backed the wrong horse, and found himself betrayed by an American in the direct employ of the President of the United States. That hurt worst of all.

It took two more passes by a fighter overhead before he was hit badly. The others had tried to hunker down as best they could, some even jumping off, but Vale stayed straight and tall for the last few minutes of his life.

On board the *Magnificent*, General Davis and Captain Manners watched the last of the lifeboats leave and watched the men die as the planes cut them down.

"I'll never live to get my revenge on Talbot Lion," Davis said regretfully. "How much time do we have?"

"Ten minutes, perhaps."

"If you have a deck of cards, we might get in a little high-stakes casino."

Manners nodded slowly. "There's a deck in my cabin."

They never made it.

"There's a lifeboat for you," Admiral Janes said. "I'll join you, of course. We have to head for Cuba."

"Hell, no," Edward Holt thundered. "I'm getting back to Washington. There's a bastard I have to see!"

"Too far in an open boat near dawn," Janes decided. "There'll be five men in the boat and if you want to fight every one of us you'll have to. And if you win, we'll go to Key West and suicide."

"In Cuba, we'll be with the fighting forces, I know," Holt said, doubtful. "I wanted to see it, but I wanted to get away, too."

"You'll agree it's probably safer out there."

Four sailors joined the VIPs in the small boat. Holt, who would have relished a *mano a mano* combat with any of the Cubans, found himself a victim of technology and not liking it. The planes passed overhead, but no bullets were snapped down at him or Janes. Exhilarated by the safety, Holt renewed his demands that the boat go to Key West. Janes, aware of the fighters overhead, shook his head firmly.

"If we start in another direction, we'll be gunned down."

Holt stared. "Are you saying that we're prisoners?"

"Yes." Janes looked over to where the *Magnificent* was going down with the others, and brushed one flipper over dry eyes. "We're prisoners, all right."

They landed on a coral beach to no sound whatever at the height of dawn. Half a dozen armed men, bearded and in fatigues, kept rifles on the new arrivals. Another man carried no weapons. He was Talbot Lion.

Edward Holt, fists at the ready, charged forward only to be pulled back by two bearded riflemen.

"Son-of-a-bitch, you played footsie with the Commies," he gasped when he could find his breath.

"I didn't want to see World War Three break out," Tal admitted. "I've arranged with these people for any of our survivors to be taken back. As for the Cubans, we've been promised that they'll be treated decently, and since I had a Russian partner in this, it'll be so."

Admiral Janes, subduing his anger, asked, "Don't you think our survivors will talk?"

"Who'll believe the people who volunteered to start World War Three? And what'll they have to be proud of?"

"Son-of-a-bitch," Holt said again. "*I'll* talk."

"No, you won't." Tal nearly smiled. "You want to be the next President, and you know there are enough Americans who feel the way I do so that you won't get any extra votes out of this trip."

"Thought of everything, haven't you?"

"As for Admiral Janes, I doubt he'll be so proud of this setback he'll want to cry on Barbara Walters' shoulder." Tal and the admiral exchanged bitter glances but understood one another.

Janes said bitterly, "And this is how Garth Crosby deals with people who don't agree with his stand."

"Spoken like a leftist," Tal chuckled, and saw the admiral's chin rise angrily. "No, this is the one way to deal with people who have the power to start World War Three and would use it illegally."

"I hope your friends in Russia will show their pacificism, but I doubt it."

"We'll keep our fingers crossed," Tal said gravely, and turned to Holt, whose silence was ominous. "My plane is parked at Baracoa airfield. I can get you to the mainland in an hour and a half, at a guess.''

Holt's response was to leap at Tal, who drew back and shouted, ''For God's sake stop it or they'll—''

Janes tried to reach the Vice President, but that, too, was in vain. The commander of the Cuban soldiers barked out a warning to the men to halt, but one of them had raised a rifle and skulled Holt. The Vice President reeled, a telltale glaze appearing in his eyes. Tal realized that the Vice President was a dead man. Janes, who wasn't facing him, rushed forward. It was a reflex action that might have cost the admiral dearly. Tal started to say, ''Knock it off!''

The admiral was so angry he didn't hear. He raised a fist to the man who had killed the Vice President. It would have been useless for Tal to interfere any further.

Another of the bearded soldiers raised a rifle and fired. Janes, a palm over his heart, dropped soundlessly to the earth at the same time as Holt did. A second shot finished Holt.

The man were glaring at Tal Lion. Tal said quietly to the commander, ''You'll remember the talks with Comrade Gurianov about the safety of any personnel who reached the mainland.''

''Accidents will happen, señor,'' said the commander, whose name was Flavio Enriquez. ''If word of this were to reach the Russian it would mean my head.''

''I will keep quiet about it,'' Tal promised easily. ''It is, after all, nothing for me to be proud of. I, too, have failed. These men are dead.''

''It was an accident,'' the commander said once more, making a sign to his men.

''Very regrettable,'' Talbot Lion said quietly. ''But accidents will happen.''

''Oh yes, señor, they will indeed.''

CHAPTER TWENTY-SIX

"Ed Holt and Admiral Janes died in a hunting accident in Montana," the President told Tal over the phone in Washington. "General Davis succumbed to diabetes. As for the CIA men, they died in the field. The sailors on the three ships are mostly all right, and will keep quiet if they want their navy careers."

"I wouldn't think that the White House could shut up so many people."

"With power, you can do a lot," Crosby said quietly. "Must've been quite a scene out there."

"It was a slice," Tal agreed. "Who's going to be the next Vice President?"

"I'm going to propose Harry Cotton's name to the Congress," Crosby said quietly. "He's CIA, and nobody would accuse me of wanting to put militarists in the saddle, so everybody will be placated. He's got brains and is a good administrator. By the way, your buddy Alva Congalton will be the head of his Secret Service detail, giving him a leg up, too, for services rendered."

Tal told himself that he'd never understand the ins and outs of so-called practical politics.

Garth added restlessly, "If only somebody could persuade Fidel to stop dumping more refugees on us than we can handle, the whole matter would've been settled satisfactorily."

Tal was wary. "Is that an assignment for me?"

"Try your hand at it, Tal," the President decided, struck

by the notion. "Diplomats haven't been able to do a damn thing, so you might."

Tal put the phone back in place and turned to Renata. They were in her room at the Hay Adams, where he had also registered. She heard his story, scowling down at the tip of a thick pencil.

"I'd have to kill Castro to get him to stop," Tal said. "I don't see any other way."

Renata looked up. "But I do."

He didn't show his surprise. "Better tell me."

"Why, it is simpleness itself. To accomplish what you did in Cuba meant the use of a partner. He is aware of owing you very much. If you remind him of how much he owes you, he should help."

"Gurianov wouldn't lift a finger, honey. The cold war is a very real antagonism and any disadvantage we have is okay with him."

"Ah, but if you also remind him that in case of another emergency, it should be possible for you and him to work together without added suspicions, then it is possible that he will see the light of day."

It was late in the afternoon when he came back to the hotel. He noticed that Renata hadn't made any sketches in the time he'd been gone, as the fresh pad hadn't been started yet. He was smiling.

"Gurianov didn't like it worth a damn, but he'll do his best and I suspect it'll work." He embraced her. "Really saved my bacon that time, girl! I owe you one for that."

"I owe you so much, too," she said quietly. "Is the President satisfied?"

"So much so that he's letting me take off for a trip and you're coming," he said. "The Caribbean okay for you?"

"The Bahamas, perhaps," she said dreamily. "A good place to do a portrait of you, Talbot. I have planned it for a long time, and you know what it will signify to me about my feelings toward you. Some preliminary sketches will be necessary, however, so you must do the one thing in the world that is hardest for you.''

"And what would that be?"

"You must sit still."

FROM THE

NICK CARTER

KILLMASTER SERIES

☐ **TEMPLE OF FEAR**	80215-X	$1.75
☐ **THE NICHOVEV PLOT**	57435-1	$1.75
☐ **TIME CLOCK OF DEATH**	81025-X	$1.75
☐ **UNDER THE WALL**	84499-6	$1.75
☐ **THE PEMEX CHART**	65858-X	$1.95
☐ **SIGN OF THE PRAYER SHAWL**	76355-3	$1.75
☐ **THUNDERSTRUCK IN SYRIA**	80860-3	$1.95
☐ **THE MAN WHO SOLD DEATH**	51921-0	$1.75
☐ **THE SUICIDE SEAT**	79077-1	$2.25
☐ **SAFARI OF SPIES**	75330-2	$1.95
☐ **TURKISH BLOODBATH**	82726-8	$2.25
☐ **WAR FROM THE CLOUDS**	87192-5	$2.25
☐ **THE JUDAS SPY**	41295-5	$1.75

Ⓒ **ACE CHARTER BOOKS**
P.O. Box 400, Kirkwood, N.Y. 13795   N-01

Please send me the titles checked above. I enclose _____.
Include 75¢ for postage and handling if one book is ordered; 50¢ per
book for two to five. If six or more are ordered, postage is free. California, Illinois, New York and Tennessee residents please add sales tax.

NAME_____

ADDRESS_____

CITY_____STATE_____ZIP_____

CHARTER BOOKS

SUSPENSE TO KEEP YOU
ON THE EDGE OF YOUR SEAT